Missing Children

Missing Children

A Novel by
HARRY H. TAYLOR

Louisiana State University Press
Baton Rouge and London   1987

Designer: Sylvia Loftin
Typeface: Meridien
Typesetter: G & S Typesetters, Inc.
Printer: Thomson-Shore, Inc.
Binder: John H. Dekker & Sons

10   9   8   7   6   5   4   3   2   1

Library of Congress Cataloging-in-Publication Data

Taylor, Harry H.
  Missing children.

  I. Title.
PS3570.A9294M47 1988   813'.54   87-22573
ISBN 0-8071-1423-5

"Affections and Unruly Wills" first appeared in the *Cimarron Review* (April, 1981), "The Wind from the Outer Shore" first appeared in *IndiAnnual II* (Fall, 1985), and "Nerves" first appeared in *Other Voices* (Fall, 1987).

Publication of this book has been supported by a grant from the National Endowment for the Arts in Washington, D.C., a federal agency.

For Barbara
For Matthew, Laurel and Sarah Elizabeth

Missing Children

1 / *Affections and Unruly Wills*

*T*hey were a close, conventional family in many ways, the five Brewster boys from Cape Cod, but when they got together with their various wives and children, somebody always broke, somebody drank too much, and then there was trouble. The brothers didn't know why this fact never occurred to them beforehand, but when they went home, when they had a reunion (always at the mother's insistence, her planning), they actually looked forward to the event with a great deal of cheerful expectation. They were going to touch base. They were returning to their roots, that windy cliff at the beginning of the New World.

When Darwin finally crossed Sagamore Bridge, when he could feel the Cape under his tires and sense the difference in the music, his heart beat more distinctly, his head cleared in the air, that fresh tang and bite. Of all five, he seemed the least rooted. He did not care about owning much, and he lived in furnished city efficiencies. He wanted to paint, and he took the kinds of menial jobs that left his days free. He was independent. If homosexual, he was cautious about his few, fairly straitlaced relationships, worried about being used, and he found himself alone more than not. He was the youngest, built like a jock, a big blond with a square jaw.

Myra Brewster, Darwin's mother, had a large, old farmhouse on lower Truro, where the narrowing Cape was treeless and breezy. She was on a hill, serene and barren, between the curving bay and the open sky, and the breezes, the odors, the lights, the shifting densities, all belonged to the sea. The house itself reflected an earlier period's concerns, and when a visitor turned a corner, some feature or characteristic reminded him of a ship. The front door opened on a narrow, dark, wintry-smelling entry; the stairs mounted sheer, like a companionway, and several windows above them resembled small portholes. Myra was from Rhode Island; she talked about returning when she retired, but at the same time, she blended in successfully with this life. She had a ship's bell on the front porch and a whale's jawbone bleaching in the front yard, covered with morning glories.

She kept three rentals, scattered around the central house like chickens around the mother hen; the two-bedroom, gray-shingled cottages brought in a sound income. Bathing suits hung on the clotheslines; stray cats picked their way through the poison ivy, and children stood on the back porches, banging the fragile screen doors, bringing in shells that smelled. The renting families themselves were not usually large; they were mostly retired couples, but they had their children up with their children, groups that camped on the pullout couches or in sleeping bags, mainly refugees from the great eastern cities as far north as Toronto or as far south as New Jersey.

A vague, soft-spoken woman who had somehow managed to weather the Cape's directness, its taciturn bite, Myra, un-like the natives, did not resent the summer people. When she sensed family problems, she brought them inspirational clip-pings from her women's magazines or the Sunday supplement sections. She found extra bedding or baked a clam pie. She seldom took from the street; she had what she called her "regulars," and when they returned to their steaming, unsafe cities, they exchanged Christmas cards.

Darwin considered her to be self-sufficient, though; and if she was lonely, if she needed these contacts, she never actu-ally said so. She was close-mouthed and private. Darwin's fa-ther had disappeared years ago, shortly after Darwin's birth, but when the captain was still, in effect, part of the family, he was usually off on a boat anyway. The sea had been his life, a cliché phrase which didn't explain much; but when he had been home, he had withdrawn from that woman's world of rentals, debts and children.

Lyle, the second oldest, still lived with her. He was her right-hand man, and he kept her overhead down. The winters were hard on the cottages. The Cape had little snow, but the wind turned serious through the winters. He patched steep roofs, repaired gutters, put in new sills and painted the trim. He was needed in many ways, and when the season opened, he was still running back and forth. Doors, windows, stuck. Steps loosened on the back stoops. The roller shades lost their springs. Toilets stopped up, and sand accumulated in the drains. He certainly did not have much free time, but as he himself said, he felt better when he kept busy.

He was, in that family, the saint, if they had a saint, and Darwin was always glad to see him. They gripped each other, and as usual, they were not afraid to hold each other. Lyle was a big boy. Darwin was big. They were all big, but Lyle was the biggest. He was also seriously overweight. Darwin decided that he looked well, despite the weight, and he said so. Lyle was on a strong, new tranquilizer, and his nails, usually bitten to the quick, were just beginning to grow back.

Lyle couldn't understand what Darwin was actually doing in New York City, or what life could be like there, other than dangerous. He did not know enough about what Darwin did to ask questions. Darwin wasn't "in" something specific, like his other brothers, like law or teaching or even public relations. On top of that, though, Lyle had been coached not to ask questions. "You're looking good, yourself," he said, anyone's health his main concern anyway. "Yes, yes, yes. Good."

They were standing alone in the empty kitchen while Lyle was making fresh coffee. "Where's everybody else?"

"You're the first in," Lyle said, beginning that running, nonstop approach of his. "Mother's down at the rentals, somewheres. You know how she is. Always going. Yes, yes, yes. She had a hard winter, too. Yes, yes, yes. She was sick a lot, you know. Did you know that? Did you?" He shook his head. "She never talks about herself, does she? Does she?" He shook his head again. "No, no, no. She wouldn't tell anyone she was sick. Right? Right, Darwin, right? She never complains. She never stops. She tires easily, too, now, but she won't admit it, and she won't stop. I keep telling her that she ought to cut back, but you know how *she* is on that subject. Right? But you can't tell her a thing, right? Other people around here don't furnish linens anymore, and I tell her *don't* furnish the linens, Ma! Don't do all that *washing*, for Christ sakes. But does she listen? Does she ever listen to us?" He was quiet for a minute, and then he bit his lower lip. "She isn't going to live forever, you know. Is she?" he concluded, as if the thought had been on his mind a lot lately.

Jerry and his wife Julia pulled in with their family, two girls from Jerry's second marriage, the baby from his third. The back doors opened as soon as the Mercedes paused, and the girls ran up on the porch to get a view of the bay. They wanted to get right down to the water, but Julia was going to have to hunt up their suits. "Hold your horses," she said, appearing with the baby next. "We have to get dug out of here." The car was filled with disposable-diaper boxes that had broken their seams, sandwich wrappings, gum paper and browning apple cores.

Darwin had trouble keeping his brothers' children's names straight and wisely did not use them. In the abstract, he liked the idea of nieces and nephews, but once around them, he felt out of his element, always vaguely excluded. His mother, in fact, had the same problem with names, and when she used a wrong name, Lyle got on her about it. He often shouted at her as if they were contemporaries, and although the others adjusted to her pleasantly mild vagueness, Lyle did not let her get away with a thing.

Jerry came out last. He looked tired, and he had lost weight. There was loose flesh around his dead-white upper arms and around the belt. He went around to the trunk, pulled the hamper out and set it against the tree to let the melting ice drain. "I can't believe it," he said, "but I've done it. I've actually brought this ship in, all hands accounted for." He had driven all the way from the West Coast. They usually flew, but since they had to pick up the girls on the way, from their mother's in the middle of the country—"in the middle," Jerry always said, "of nowhere, literally"—flying had not worked out well, with the lack of connections.

"Where's your problem?" Julia asked. "You just drove." She was a tall, freckled woman with long, calfless legs.

They were still standing around in the yard. There was always that moment, between the car and the house, before everybody could pull himself up out of this particular kind of separateness. "I'm still on the road," Jerry said. He draped his big arm around both brothers, briefly. "How's the little brother?" he asked Darwin. "How's the jock?" Darwin grinned uncomfortably. He had once worked out, back in high school, when he had been completely centered on himself, before painting, and Jerry kept up this running joke. They moved slowly toward the house. "Smell that air, Julia, just smell it. Well? Is it good to be up here, or not?"

Lyle entered the house first, on his way to the refrigerator, worried about lunch. He moved bottles around inside. "Where's Ma, anyway? Should we start without her? We're all getting pretty hungry, right? Isn't everybody getting hungry? Doesn't everybody want to eat? Yes, yes, yes! It's time to eat."

"I'm not particularly hungry yet," Julia said. She lit a cigarette while she changed the baby on the kitchen table, and Jerry found her a dish. Myra did not keep ashtrays in the house because she said ashtrays just encouraged smokers. Julia wanted to get into her suit, too. When she spotted water, she wanted to touch up her tan as soon as she could. She spent the summertime there on the beach with half an eye on the children, guarding her cigarettes and her glass against their exertions. "Watch the cigarettes," she said, every five minutes. "Don't step on Julia's cigarettes and watch that drink."

The two girls were still on the porch when Myra showed up. The family could hear the girls' shouting, sounding false, too hearty, and then her low murmur. She appeared in the kitchen carrying soiled linen, and as usual, she resembled an eccentric servant. She was in the captain's baseball cap and a torn T-shirt that advertised a local health food shop. Darwin and Jerry embraced her by turns while she kept her arms around the sheets, and then she bent down to give her new grandchild an appraising look. She was searching for a family feature, a familiar sign. "Oh, he's so *small*," she said, finally giving up. Then she was off, squeezing sideways through the utility room door with the sheets. Lyle had built the addition, room for the ironing board, the washer and dryer, the metal shelves kept filled with freshly stacked linen. She returned empty-handed.

Jerry was holding the recently changed baby while Julia fixed a bottle. He moved it up and down gently against his chest, keeping it happy with this rocking movement. "Mother? Julia write you I was in TV now?"

"I wrote, yes. How's the painting going, Darwin? Any big commissions yet?"

Darwin flushed over the attention paid. "I'm not cut out for big commissions," he said.

"I lost weight," Jerry said, patting his stomach, glancing at his wife for confirmation. "I thought, well, why not? Slim down for the job interviews if I don't look in my twenties these days."

"I don't pay much attention to people's appearances," Myra said, reflectively. "Every time, it's up above that counts."

"I wouldn't put down any big commission, myself," Jerry said.

Lyle was bending over a dripping head of lettuce at the sink. "*Ma!* I can't find the mayonnaise. Didn't you buy any *mayonnaise?* How am I going to fix lunch without mayonnaise?"

"It's there. Just look, before it bites you. On the top shelf. If it were a snake, it would bite you. My! Can't we have a pleasant lunch? Can't we have a nice, pleasant lunch without all this *fuss?*"

He moved the bottles around until they found the mayonnaise, and he pulled out the ham.

Myra was still standing in the middle of all the activity with the baseball cap on backwards. "That ham's for supper. We're having the tuna fish for lunch."

He turned, still holding the ham. "Christ, I've been looking at the ham all morning! Why can't we have it now? Doesn't anybody else want the ham now? Ask your guests. Yes, yes, yes! Ask *them! They'll* tell you!"

"We're having tuna fish for lunch. Everybody wants the tuna fish for lunch."

Myra kept them abreast of the tenants' lives over the iced tea and tuna fish salad. She could recognize the cars as soon as they pulled off the road. She had six sets, three who appeared in July and three in August: first the Maplewoods, the Coles and the Hendersons, and then the Donaldsons, the Gilberts and the Tapleys. She discussed their various allergies and illnesses, their successes and defects, their domestic problems and their children's setbacks.

Charley and his wife appeared while the family was still having lunch. Charley was Charley; he came in talking. Misty was pregnant, her first, just starting to fill out, a small, spare gently curved girl, closer to Darwin's age than anyone else's there, and when Darwin had first met her, he had been prepared to ignore some kind of unspoken sexual pressure, but she was uncomplicated, good natured. She took the world at face value. When males sometimes approached, she did not recognize these advances, the sudden shifts in tones and textures. Neither sullenness nor guile nor outright lust had seemed to touch her yet.

They had stopped on the road to eat, but Lyle found extra kitchen chairs because he wanted everybody around the table. He loved having the family together, in one spot. He had everybody move over, and he pulled the chairs up. He fussed, fixing more iced tea.

"Well," Charley asked, toward Jerry, "How's the West Coast world? How's Walt Disney doing?" They were both rhetorical questions, and Jerry didn't answer. Charley knew, anyway, that Jerry was in Washington, not California.

Misty looked tired, on edge. "Disney's dead," she said, in Charley's general direction.

Charley didn't answer her. They had obviously been quarreling. He was a good deal older than Misty, and when he married her, his first marriage, he was already in his middle forties. He was, by then, a full professor with a lot of publishing credits behind him, and if he was happy where he was, in a small college in southern Ohio, the bucolic atmosphere was partly deceiving, because his students could do undergraduate work in the Yoruba and Kiswahili languages. The tuition was formidable.

He had drunk heavily during his graduate student days; stories still circulated, but some foolishness or waywardness must have been bred out of him through the years, because he now concentrated on his career. He ran seminars on Robert Graves and the goddess in all her various manifestations. He specialized in her mother role, and during his last three years on campus, the last two with a government grant, he chaired an annual spring conference on the subject. He brought in scholars from both coasts and put them up for two weeks on federal money. These professionals (some anthropologists, but mostly literary people) read papers, watched films and attended panel discussions. Charley's marriage, or at least his life, struck people as ideal. Misty's father had left her a little money. They had an old farmhouse on several acres, once a cow pasture. They owned a stream, a clump of willows, and a small pond. They flew to London for Christmas, and they spent time in Europe in the late spring.

Charley was still brooding over Misty's put-down. "Walt Disney can't die. He's just transfigured. Living in Donald Duck."

Misty ignored him. "He always has to be right," she said, to the room in general.

"Oh, that's just a male," Julia said, a favorite phrase of hers which could include a certain amount of goodwill.

Charley frowned. "Women close around women during these times, a special club."

"Well, it's a special time."

Myra stirred the iced tea, rattling the cubes around in her glass. "Can't we have a pleasant meal, folks? Why can't we have a *pleasant* meal?"

"That's right," Lyle said. "We're all together now, aren't we?"

"It's pleasant, Mother," Charley said. "Who said it isn't pleasant?"

Misty didn't drop the subject. She was telling Julia about her monthly checkups. "I love them because I make a day of it. I have lunch in town and see a movie afterwards."

"Charley ought to be with you. I dragged Jerry along when I had mine."

"Dragged?" Jerry said. "I don't remember any dragging."

"I dragged."

Charley cleared his throat. "I went once. The doctor wanted me to hear the heartbeat."

"I remember the heartbeats," Jerry said.

"I leaned down, close to the belly, dutifully, as so instructed, but I could only hear a general roar through the instrument. Could have been, for all I know, jungles in there, whole civilizations."

"I'm not sure this is table conversation," Myra said.

"Oh, I see!" Lyle said, "I get it! Misty's pregnant!"

Julia's baby started to cry, and Myra looked around. "Who's crying?" she asked, half-kidding, addressing the baby directly in the portable car seat at Julia's feet. "Who's crying? Who's making all that noise? Who's putting up such a *fuss?*"

Darwin saw Julia's face harden. His mother wasn't young, but she was still independent and self-sufficient, and if she needed to see her family every so often, she made no great claims on anyone. Given this, then, why couldn't everybody bear with her few eccentricities? Why couldn't everyone be pleasant?

"What shall we do, Mother?" Jerry asked. "Should Julia put him down?"

Julia picked up the baby. "Oh, you've got your life cut out for you now, Misty. Never a dull moment."

Everybody got up. Myra drifted off into the utility room to start the washer. Lyle ran dishwater. Darwin and Jerry helped. "That's it, that's it," Lyle said, "everybody pitches in. That's right. There's always something that needs doing around here. No rest for the weary, right? Am I right?"

Julia and the two girls returned in bathing suits. "Keep your ear out, will you, Jerry? He's down. He'll sleep, I think, but hold the fort while I work on this tan."

Lyle was stacking the sudsy, dripping dishes. "Well," he said to Jerry, "what do we have here, a sun worshiper?" He did not know what to make of her, a West Coast exotic, and he usually addressed Jerry's wife through Jerry.

"I don't worship the sun, exactly, but I like a good tan, and when I'm really brown, I worship that."

"She's pretty smart, too, isn't she, Jerry?" he said when she had left. "I bet you have to get up early to beat her."

"I couldn't *get* up early enough."

They could hear Myra moving something back in the utility room, and Lyle turned around with a dish in his hand. "*Mother!* Get out of that *hot* utility room, for *Christ* sakes!" His face was red, rounded and puffy. She couldn't hear over the washing machine, and he shook his head. "What's going to happen when she can't cut the mustard any more? What's going to happen then? Tell me that!"

Darwin wanted a short nap, but once upstairs he could not sleep. At the open windows the breezes blew the shades back and forth, slapping them against the sills. The sun was still piercing at four, like high noon, perfect for browning or burning, but he couldn't get his cigarette lit in these strong, salty cross breezes.

He was in his old bedroom, and when he studied himself in the familiar mirror, standing sideways in his briefs, he was doing so for old times' sake; the eighteen-year-old body builder was missing. Remembering him was like remembering someone with whom he had had an affair, years and years back, a stranger.

Jason arrived below, with his boys, but Darwin lingered, enjoying the solitude. Jason was the success in the family, or at least the one who made the most money. He was a tax lawyer, but because his work was sedentary, he jogged a lot. He ran in all weathers and in all places, and when he pulled in off the road, he came upstairs to climb into his jogging shorts. Darwin could hear him in the bedroom next door.

He was divorced, but he had his children in August, two quiet, curiously well-mannered boys, younger than Jerry's two girls. When Darwin went down, the boys were sitting on the edges of the furniture trying to make conversation in a house which was essentially filled with strangers.

Darwin and Jerry took the boys down to the beach. They did not feel entirely comfortable with them. They were hoping to run into Julia and the two girls, but they only found their beach blankets. They had gone for a walk. The four sat down on the blankets, and after the day's various tensions, Darwin tried to relax. The tide was in. The late afternoon heat was still like midday in its intensity, but the quality of the light was different. Cottages and white boats stood out as if freshly painted, and the cloudless sky was luminous.

Jason came toward them. He was running along the edges of the water, and when he reached them, he dropped down on the sand close to their blankets. He removed his T-shirt. He was thinning on top, but otherwise hairy; he had hair across his shoulders in back. Like his brothers Jerry and Lyle, he was inclined toward fat, and despite his jogging, he kept a thick, rubbery-looking waist. He was breathing heavily, if not panting, and he wiped his face and his arms with his shirt. "Running on sand, even hard sand like this, isn't the same," he said. "I'm going to have to build to it." He watched Darwin lighting a cigarette. Darwin could tell he did not approve, but at the same time he wasn't going to say anything.

"Well, how's everything going with everybody? Myra tells me you've changed jobs, Jerry."

Jerry nodded, uncomfortable under the scrutiny. "I'm in Seattle at the moment. I'm in television."

Jason knit his brows. He waited, trying to understand. "Are you in acting?"

Jerry moved his foot, pulling it up under the other. "Acting? Me? Good Lord, no!"

"Just what, then, exactly, do you do now?"

"Oh, a little of this, a little of that. Public relations, mostly. The same game."

"What's the security like? What are the long-term benefits?"

"I'm working on these problems."

Jason frowned. "Don't people usually settle those matters *before* they take the job?" But Darwin had his turn. "How's the painting going these days?" Jason asked, the tone heartier, less interested, as if he did not intend to pursue this line of questioning.

Darwin merely said, "Fine," as if he were amused, but was not.

"Let up, Jason," Jerry said. "We're on vacation." He was looking at the sky, which was still holding that clear, pure light. "It's a renewal, just being back."

Jason finally nodded, and when Jerry repeated himself, the children nodded, too. They sat there on the blanket, staring at the sea politely.

When they came up from the bay, Charley was fixing drinks in the parlor, where the general conversation was animated and pleasant. They all had those times when, for a few moments, the family circle seemed real enough, its warmth substantial; and partly because of the drinks, partly because they were together again after a long absence, they were in their different ways trying to be supportive.

Jason asked Charley about his work. Jason was the kind who could never understand just what an English teacher does, precisely, but, in his brother's case, he was further thrown off-balance because of Charley's specialty. He did not know anything about the goddess, of course, but he also could not imagine what there *could* be there to consume an adult's attention. Jason wanted to get along that evening, though, and when he asked Charley about his spring conferences, the overture was touching.

Charley was shy at first, just because touched, but while he was freshening his drink, he launched into the subject. He was surprisingly good with figures. He had more of a business head on him than people supposed, and, once into administration and government money, he appeared to thrive on the red tape.

Julia looked impressive that evening in a new silk blouse and a severe pants suit. She didn't get to the East Coast often, and when she did, she expected to enjoy herself. She expected to get out. She asked Lyle about places they ought to see on the Cape. She wanted to know about the sights, and if he was reclusive, if he didn't get around much, he was trying to be helpful.

His expression gradually changed, though, and he started to shake his head. "I don't know much about what's going on these days. But everything's *changing* around here, Jerry," he said, turning to him. "Yes, yes, yes! You wouldn't believe it! The towns, the traffic, the beaches. Oh, yes! Even the beaches!"

Julia waited, interested, but he didn't go on. "Why? What's up?"

He was still shaking his head. "You wouldn't want to take your children around some of these beaches!" He left the room.

Misty came down last. She had been soaking in a hot tub, and she looked considerably freshened after the trip. She had her hair up, revealing her small ears and the long, clear, thin neck. She was carrying the child high, and while she looked down at her shape, she seemed to be alone with herself. When Charley brought her a drink, she dreamily stared into space.

Jerry noticed the glow, that transient sense of well-being. "You're going through a wonderful period in your life," he said.

She glanced at him without smiling, without answering, but her expression deepened, as if he had hit on something, some view, she had not yet fully considered. They seemed united for a second, cut off from the group.

Charley cleared his throat, and Darwin waited, worried about what was coming next. He froze, feeling out of his element. "Too bad you were spared motherhood, Jerry."

The semiprivacies and silences and long, sweeping griefs of these heterosexual existences could surface in a minute, when Darwin was least expecting it. "Oh, shut up, Charley," he said, too stridently, sounding queer.

Myra appeared. "I could use some help, getting this show on the road. How about it? Chop, chop." The women followed her back out.

Myra wanted the children fed separately, and while she set the table in the kitchen, using her best china in there, too, putting a linen napkin beside each plate, the women looked at each other without anything specific *to* do. The men wandered back and forth with their drinks.

Lyle needed these leisurely moments; he needed the family, and he told them how he looked forward to these weeks all year. However, he was also a creature of habit, and he was beginning to fret. He wanted to know when they were going to eat. He liked meals on time. He wanted to move right along. Besides, he did not drink, partly because of the strong pills he took, and while the brothers stood around with their glasses, he kept opening the oven door to check on the ham. "You aren't going to let it burn, are you? It's done now, isn't it? Isn't it? Isn't it ready to take out? Yes, yes, yes! It's ready to take out!"

"Take it easy," she kept saying. "Just hold your horses."

He started to fuss around the children's table, and he brought in more chairs than he needed. "Where do you want everybody to sit? Mother? *Ma?* Where do you want everybody placed?"

In any event, during one of these trips, he moved the green portable car seat, with the baby, and the baby started to cry.

Myra turned around. "Who's crying now? Who's crying? Who's setting up all that *fuss?*"

Julia picked the baby up. "He won't sleep around the clock, you know. So? Where do you want him now dumped?"

Jerry instantly looked unhappy. "Julia!"

Myra didn't answer. She just pursed her mouth, slightly. She always told everyone that she just ignored people's sarcasm, for the sake of peace. She said she could not get angry. She just never could.

Lyle turned white. He looked from Myra to Julia without saying a word, and nobody spoke. He stood in the middle of the crowded kitchen, hunched over, biting his nails. "*Jesus* Christ!" he finally said, under his breath.

For all the secretiveness, there was little actual privacy in that place. Darwin lay awake that night listening to Jerry and Julia arguing through the thin walls. The house was like a sieve.

"What's the point, after all, in unpleasantness?" Jerry was

saying. "Mother doesn't always notice what she says, or what it sounds like when she says it. She's her own person, in many ways, I'll admit, but she needs her family around her for a few weeks, and while we're here, we try to overlook her faults. What's the point in not?"

"Faults, you say. *I'll* say she has faults!"

Julia didn't go on for a minute, and Darwin lay there listening to the tide coming in, washing against the rocks. Farther down the hall someone coughed.

"She rolls the family around and shakes it up as if she's rolling dice around in a cup. However, at the same time, *she* wouldn't admit what she was doing for a second. *Butter wouldn't melt in her mouth.*"

"Now, baby," Jerry said, "you're overreacting. Aren't you overreacting, just a bit? She's actually a serene sort of person."

"Well, if so, her serenity sets my teeth on edge. You can think what you want to, of course, but *I* think she's just a little crazy. *I* happen to think she's just this side of bonkers."

Jerry kept his voice lower. He said something that Darwin could not catch, and she said, "Besides, none of you makes much sense. You don't. *I've* seen the looks you've given Charley's wife. The *two* of you, mooning like monks in outer space, as if nobody's ever been pregnant before. She isn't helpless. Actually, if you ask me, she's a lot more willful than anyone around *here* happens to contemplate."

Moisture webbed the screens in the early morning hours, and haze soaked the scrub. While they waited for the ribbons of fog to burn off, Darwin and Jason gathered the children's buckets, shovels and blankets. Then, around ten o'clock, when they had the party organized, they went down the trail single file toward the water in the contrasting clarity, the fresh, pristine light.

Jerry's two girls, older, louder, more confident, gradually took over Jason's two boys. Impressed, quiet, the boys allowed themselves to be ordered around a lot.

Darwin and Jason set up camp while they kept their eyes on the children. They finally carried their first catch up out of the water: four children bent over a dripping bucket, staring down at whatever they'd managed to separate from the sea, a haunting image because so immemorial.

Jason stayed formal with the boys, as if they were small adults, but once that morning, in a moment of weakness, he told his younger brother what his divorce had cost him. "Do you know the hardest thing I do these days?" he asked him. "I have to give the boys up when September comes. It gets worse all the time."

Charley started drinking earlier than usual that day. Jason tried to ignore the fact, which wasn't easy to do, given Charley's soft, unfocused look. Jason was still on the morning's subject, the importance of the family. "Well, old man," he said, "your life's going to change now, isn't it? Bound to, once you have kids."

Darwin saw problems coming. Charley called Jason Saint Leviticus behind his back. However, Charley was off on his own train of thought. "Has me, already," he said.

"Nothing like children. Nothing like the whole process. Bound to mature anybody, some."

"I went through a restless period when Misty first got pregnant. I fell on her after lunch, and I fell on her again at night."

Darwin didn't want to hear this, and Jason flushed with anger.

"Couldn't make a dent, though. I still felt overstimulated after sex, as if I hadn't actually accomplished that much."

"You ought to be counting your blessings," Jason said.

"Interesting story here, and I'll tell it. The woman's always thinking ahead. The woman has her eye on the future, where it's at, and once she's found the male, any nice male, she's already beyond *him*. Why, by then, he's just so much dead weight."

The family was taking Myra out for dinner, and Julia showed up first, already dressed. "What's going on now? Why is everybody looking so glum? Are we going to spend another night in, or what?"

They took two cars: Julia, Jerry, Darwin and Jason in his, the others in Lyle's. Jason followed Lyle up onto Route Six, away from Provincetown.

Julia suddenly sat up straighter. "Where we are headed? Aren't we going into town? Aren't we allowed to see the sights?"

"Take it easy," Jerry said. "Lyle doesn't like the P-town crowds."

"Well, then, why did I bother to dress up?"

"Mother's chosen the place. Aren't we supposed to be taking her out?"

They ate in a Chinese restaurant on the highway. The family ordered drinks in the orange glow. Given the special occasion, Lyle had a drink, too. He ordered a strawberry daiquiri but never finished it.

"This isn't bad, is it, Julia?" Jerry said.

Julia's face was stiff. "Why, it's perfect."

Lyle didn't pick up the tensions between them. He was wearing a new checkered sport shirt under his plaid jacket, the shirt collar buttoned to the neck. "It's still a family place, Julia. You can bring your family here. Yes, yes, yes!" He shook his head. "Now *some* of these places," he said, without finishing his sentence.

The service was slow, and while they were waiting, Charley ordered another drink. When the food came, he pushed his water glass back and moved his drink in closer. He seemed to be shut off somewhere, and when he talked to Misty, he appeared to forget the others. He was against her nursing, and he wouldn't drop the subject. "There are, you know, two sides to this whole business."

Misty's easygoing quality was missing. "You're going to have to learn to share me," she said, too matter-of-factly, the voice cold.

He leaned toward her across the table, just missing his drink. "I can share! I can share! I can share! I can learn to share, for Christ sakes! That's not the problem! Just don't cut me out, Misty!"

"Oh, *Charley!* We're in *public!* Just *drop* it, *will* you?"

Lyle started to fidget. The rest kept a neutral conversation going.

Since Myra's rentals were turning over soon, she was already preoccupied with the changes. The Maplewoods, the Coles and the Hendersons were getting ready to leave, the Hendersons starting back early to get ahead of the traffic during the turnover period. She was waiting for the Donaldsons, the Gilberts and the Tapleys. The Donaldsons were bringing children, the Gilberts their children and grandchildren, one, a boy, autistic. The Tapleys were childless and lingered over Labor Day. He owned two florist shops, and, filled with Old World ways, they always brought her a plant.

"They buy a new car every year," Myra said, "but I always know who's arriving when they swing past the house. The plant's back there, wedged in among the luggage. They're *so* thoughtful. They never forget."

"Why *should* they forget?" Julia asked, actually trying to get along. "I bet you spoil *them* rotten."

Darwin could see trouble coming. "They spoil each other," he said.

"Now, Julia," Jerry said.

Lyle glanced up. "That's right. That's right! Yes, yes, yes. *You* tell her, Julia! I can't. She won't listen to me. She works too hard. Never stops."

"She chooses her own life, Lyle," Darwin said.

"Oh, yes," Julia remarked, determined to go on. "Sometimes an in-law can say what others can't."

Myra looked away. She tightened her mouth a little.

"Act like a workhorse, and people will treat you like a workhorse."

"Mother can take care of herself," Jason said, firmly. "She always could."

Lyle rolled his eyes and pushed back his chair. The meal over, he was ready to get going. "She's always on her feet," he said.

"Why don't you get married, like your brothers?" Myra said. "Why don't you find your *own* house?"

Lyle didn't answer. Darwin couldn't see his face. He turned, on his way out.

Misty was trying to get Charley moving, but he was still involved in his own thoughts. "Listen," he said. "I've just had a great idea! Why don't we divide up what the baby can have and what I can have? That's fair enough, isn't it? That's simple justice. Just don't *nurse*. After all, they're *my* breasts. I found them first!"

Darwin lay awake listening to Jerry and Julia arguing in the room next door again. They finally fell asleep, but the after-effects of so much unpleasantness kept him awake much longer. He lay listening to the shades flapping against the sills. He heard Jason next, coughing in the back room where he was sleeping with his sons. Then Myra got up to use the bathroom. She must have partly woken Jason because he opened his door a crack. "Who is it? Who is it?" he asked, sounding half-asleep. "Who is it? Dad? Dad? Are you *back?* Are you home?"

Darwin finally fell asleep. He had cloudy, anxious dreams: trains missed, a painting dissolving, important papers stolen, children mislaid or lost, and when he woke, shortly after dawn, he was still moving through those webby, shadowy feelings.

He drove over to Herring Cove to clear his head, parked in the public lot and set off on foot across the sand toward the lighthouse.

First, there was the family stretch: normal bathing, normal sunning, and everybody legally covered. When he reached the less crowded sections, he started to run into a topless woman or two, here and there, in among the fully suited. On principle, people did not pay the topless particular attention, and there was something still curiously mannered about the scene, as if a few, just a few, were trying out a new fad ahead of time.

Farther on, where the wild grass on his left grew thicker and the salt ponds increased, he ran into topless lesbians who were embracing each other in plain sight. They seemed less sexually involved than consciously on exhibit, an experiment, trying out whatever they needed to try out, and then he reached the gay males who were playing catch without their trunks.

All this, as he passed, struck him as some sort of weary pilgrimage, as if all his normal goodwill were being tested. The lighthouse seemed no closer, and he decided to turn back.

When he entered the house, the place was quiet, the downstairs deserted. Starting upstairs, on his way to the shower, he ran into Lyle. Lyle knew where he had been because he said nothing. For once, he did not ask any questions.

They ate dinner early that evening. Lyle was going into town to get a prescription filled. He didn't want to go alone, and he was trying to find someone to ride in with him. Lyle wasn't simpleminded, really. He knew he was supposed to be tolerant, and in a sense he was, but he sensed in the summer Provincetown forces some form of disintegration which was just too much for him. After all, the Cape was still his home.

Charley didn't want to go. He was fixing himself a drink. He wasn't terribly steady, and when he saw Jason looking at him with disapproval, he toasted his health. "Here we go, Jason. Bottoms up. Waste not, want not."

Jason was clearly disgusted. "You don't know what you have going for you, a beautiful young woman like that and a child on the way. You just don't realize what you have going for you."

"Old Jason. Just look at him. The master of his soul, the captain of his fate. You're up to your ass in free will, aren't you?"

"You ought to be counting your blessings instead of hitting the bottle."

Lyle was standing hunched over, biting his nails, his eyes darting back and forth between them. "Now, Jason," he kept saying, "please! Jason! Be pleasant! Please!"

Darwin was petrified. He did not know what to do.

In the past they had all tried to be pleasant around Lyle. They had all pretty much protected him, but Jason turned on him now. "My God, just *look* at you! *Living* on pills!"

Charley stumbled forward. "Just a *minute, Jason!"*

Jason turned on him. "You're all weaklings. You live on booze. Jerry runs from job to job, from woman to woman. And what's Darwin doing, besides just drifting?"

Charley leaned against Jason's chest and pushed. Jason stepped back, trying to get away from him, but in reflex he put his fist up, ready to take a swing at his brother if necessary. However, he couldn't get a clean punch in because Charley fell against his chest again.

Lyle pulled the two apart and stepped between them. He was huge: huge shoulders, huge chest, huge stomach. He was bigger than any of them, and they were all pretty big boys. He was also afraid of violence, and he was shaking now. He was trembling so he had trouble speaking. "CUT IT OUT! CUT IT OUT! JUST CUT IT OUT, YOU TWO!"

He was unusually quiet on the trip into town. Darwin could sense in the silence a growing, enervating depression that could wipe his brother out for weeks at a time. He didn't try to comfort him, though. What could he say? What would be the use?

They parked just off Bradford. They crossed Bradford on foot and cut down through an alley into town.

Lyle finally broke the silence. "Jason's right, Darwin."

"No, he isn't, Lyle. Jason's never right."

"Why did we get into that, with our mother around?"

"She wasn't around."

"She was down at the cottages. She could *hear* us! She could hear *me,* all over!"

They reached lower Commercial, where the fun starts, where the tasteless cut-rate stores and the fast-food places begin. The accumulation of smells was overwhelming: the pizza, the clam rolls, the French fries and chocolate fudge bubbling in vats. There was also grass around, its sweetish odors just detectable beneath the others. The crowds, at seven, were already heavy. They were milling around through the bumper-to-bumper traffic in the middle of the narrow, one-way street. A few annoyed drivers, obviously unaccustomed to the town's ways, honked at the pedestrians, but the walkers did not bother to look up, much less move. The cars waited, inched gradually forward, looking for parking places which did not exist.

"He's right, Darwin. But I *have* to live on these pills, don't I?"

"Oh, yes. He knows that."

They were on the walk, at first, but because of the weaving packs, they were soon in the street. They fought through the standard tourist crowds, the grandmothers in tight knit slacks, bare stomachs, bare backs. These people were still in the majority, but they also passed two young men in denims holding hands, two middle-aged women in capes, their arms across each others' hips, a bearded, elderly male with gold loops in his ears, his shorts so spare they outlined the bulging groin. He was talking to a young traffic cop on duty.

A family unit stood huddled together just outside the drugstore, ringed with the traffic which always reminded Darwin of boyhood Halloweens in small towns. The father was tall, thin and untanned. He was in plaid Bermuda shorts, knee-high socks and black loafers. He was passing out sticks of gum to his wife and three children. Removed from the crowd, isolated inside the fragile family circle, he appeared to be less disapproving than determined to hold out against the surrounding flux. "One for you," he was saying, holding the gum out, "one for you, one for you, and one for you." He took the last.

It started to drizzle on the way back. The rain soon came down harder, finally a heavy, gray, screening wall, and when the windshield wipers couldn't handle the weather any longer, Lyle pulled over just before he reached the open bay. He raised his hands from the wheel, and in the half-dark, he looked at Darwin helplessly. He just shook his head. He was crying. He was weeping without making any sound, but his shoulders were shaking.

Darwin actually had his own griefs, and under their various pressures, he felt removed, cut off. What could he do? He loved Lyle, didn't he? So he held him. They held each other for a moment without speaking, brother against brother. When the storm passed, they released each other. They went on.

2 / The Wind from the Outer Shore

Jerry was having problems at work that winter. The faction that sided with him was less powerful than the faction that did not, and when his faction finally began to dwindle further, he found himself out on the street.

Since he did not want the world to know that he was down when he was down, he decided to spruce up. He joined a good club and he bought some clothes. He turned his small gray Mercedes in on a large white Mercedes.

Jason was on the phone in late April while Jerry was still job hunting. Jason was trying to make summer plans, but Jerry couldn't be definite. However, he said nothing about his troubles because there was no sense going into details.

Charley called him next. "Look, Jerry," he said, jumping right into his news, "you're going to hear all this sooner or later. Misty had a miscarriage, and things haven't been up to snuff lately." Jerry tried to express appropriate sympathy, but Charley interrupted him. "I called Myra, of course. Had to, didn't I? Can't lie about that," he concluded, considering the brothers' need to shield their mother from the facts. "There's either a grandchild on the way, or there isn't. In this case there isn't. She took it well, too. You know her. There was a moment's silence, and then she said, 'Well, Misty's still young.'"

"That's true, Charley. Misty's still got plenty of time."

"Well, as a matter of fact, there's a lot more to all this than that. She generally hasn't been herself. She was depressed a lot, through that whole period. She finally left me. She's with her mother. They're both Catholics, and you can't make a dent. Anyway, they're on tour together, thick as thieves, seeing Europe."

Jerry decided he was getting less than half the story. "You both could use some counseling, Charley. A good man could sort this out."

"Look. I'm not going into all this with Myra. I'm just saying Misty's with her mother in Europe, seeing the museums and getting her strength back. No sense in telling more than I have to at the moment."

Jerry considered telling Charley about his own troubles, but he changed his mind. "Are you going up this summer, then?"

"Why," Charley asked, catching something in the tone, "aren't you? We have to, don't we?"

"In fact, a lot of things in my life are pretty fluid right now."

"Through the grapevine I heard that Darwin had a rough winter. A lot of flu, you know—in one way or another—and he was out of work. Well, a good Samaritan appeared, apparently off the street, and nursed him back to health. Then he wouldn't leave. Stuck to him like glue. Stole, I guess, and ran up some bills."

"My God, Charley, he's the little brother! We ought to keep in touch."

"Tried calling, of course, but he'd moved. Wouldn't know what to say, anyway, would I? He's just like her, when you think about it. A very private, very self-sufficient person. They both have their secrets."

"Hard sometimes to know what he wants. I know that any of us would do anything we could."

"Don't mention any of this to Myra. Don't mention it to Darwin, either."

"That's right. I always let him bring up what he wants to, himself. If not, then not."

"I don't know what else to do, myself," Charley said.

Myra called next. She mentioned the miscarriage first, briefly, to get the bad news out of the way. "We won't bring it up again," she said, as if the news were their little secret. "They can have more, anyway, can't they?" She would not want to hear about Charley's marriage troubles. She wanted the status quo, and considering her age, he understood the need for carefully preserved surfaces. They discussed the weather and her rentals, and then she abruptly changed the subject. She told him that Jason had said he'd been evasive about his summer plans.

The statement was, for her, an unusually oblique remark, and it took him off guard. "Evasive? Evasive? I don't remember being evasive. Why would I be evasive?" He told her he was coming.

Lyle called. He sounded as if he sensed problems. Jerry kept his troubles away from Lyle, too, because he was such a worrier. And when he started to worry—worry about anything, in fact—he had to talk. He had to worry the problem through aloud, and when he started doing this, he carried what he knew back to Myra. He finally had to tell her everything. "Are you *sure* everything's okay?" he asked, several times. "You're all right? Julia's all right? You're coming out, aren't you?" Jerry continued to reassure him. "Well, just checking. Just let me know when you want me to meet the plane."

Jerry would be driving again, this time to save expenses. "I'll have the car, Lyle."

And that alerted him. "Driving? Driving? Driving? Yes, yes, yes? In your car? In your car? All the way? That's a long way, isn't it? Isn't it, right?" Then he stopped, for a second, before he made his point. "You told me you'd never drive across the country again. That's what you said, last time."

Myra's place was perched up on the treeless, open moors, but given the hills and hammocks, the tucks and sudden bends, the big, weathered farmhouse loomed up at the last minute. Myra and Lyle had just gotten back from shopping, and Lyle was unloading the pickup.

When he saw the car, he paused, both arms filled with shopping bags. He put the bags down again in the back of the truck. "*Geesus*," he exclaimed, his pale blue eyes huge with delight. When he went over, crossing as quickly as he could, he brushed his palms against his thighs as if they were soiled, as if he couldn't be clean enough for the greeting.

"A new car, Jerry, right, right? A new car? You got a new car? Is *that* why you wanted to drive again? Is it? Is it? I don't blame you. No, no, no! That's a *big* Mercedes, isn't it? Isn't it? Isn't that a bigger Mercedes than you had before? Yes, yes, yes! That's a bigger Mercedes than you had before. Boy! You must be doing *good* out there on the Coast, Jerry, right? You must be doing great! Well, come on, then. Let's not stand around here. Let's go in. Yes, yes, yes! Let's not stand around here all day!"

He wanted to leave the groceries, but they carried them in together while Julia held the door. "Yes, yes, yes! That's it! That's it! Everybody works around here. No rest for the weary, right? Right, Jerry, right? Isn't that the way it is at your place?" He shook his head, delighted with his predicament. "I *tell* you! Boy! It's *good* to keep busy, though, right? I keep busy all the time. There's always something that needs doing here. Takes your mind off yourself, though, right? No sense dwelling on things," he said, shaking his head. "Is there?" He set the groceries down on the kitchen table. "Right? Right? No, no, no, that's not good!"

Myra was stocking the freezer. "Do you know one of our great failings?" she said, over her shoulder, while the family milled around the kitchen: Jerry's two from his previous marriage, Julia with their boy. Jerry had not stopped, once he had hit the Cape, and they all needed bathrooms. "Oh, I *wish* we didn't have one of our great weaknesses." Myra turned for a moment to make her point. "We have to eat, don't we? We have to eat if we want to stay alive. Let me just get this *food* put away—all parts of animals—and then we're going to play a little game. Everybody is going to tell about *one* memorable thing that happened to him or her this year. That goes for the children, too. Children? Now you be *thinking*. You be ready!" She turned to Julia, who was herding them toward the bathroom in back. "Oh, these *children*, they're all so *new*, so *minted*," she observed, in bewilderment, seeing more than there were. "They're all little *poems!*"

26

"Oh, yes, Myra! But all these little poems have bladders."

Jerry wandered around, needing to stretch, trying to get his bearings back in the old place. He found Charley in the front parlor.

Charley had just returned from one of his many meditative hikes—out there alone with his drink in the distance at low tide, stopping at favorite spots up to his ankles, then perched on a sandbar, among the gulls, his back to the shoreline. When his glass was empty, the gin-soaked lime peel lying at the bottom in the grit, he hoisted himself up, starting back, toward more gin.

Charley was in before dinner, between his afternoon drinks and his evening drinks (gin, gin and more gin). He was working on a fresh drink now, his soiled T-shirt rich, smelling like a good *bouillabaisse*. He still had that sloping, energetic, side-to-side gait, before the drinking picked up. He moved as if he were full of life, with atoms to burn, and his speech had not yet begun to blur.

He wanted to talk about his marriage for a moment, but since the phone call, his angle of vision on the subject had changed slightly. "Misty and I have separated," he said without hesitation, as if he were now sure of his version. "A mutual agreement, a common pact. Everybody very sensible, very civilized. Understanding and forgiveness on both sides. A lot of serious hugging and kissing all around, in a kind of relieved way, like saved sinners. A page turned, in everybody's lives."

Jerry did not know what to say, exactly. "That's a shame."

"I'm not, though, you know, telling the others, just yet."

Lyle stopped by, heading into town on an errand, and he wanted company. Jerry decided to go. While Lyle was looking for his keys, Jerry got out the Mercedes. His brother stood on the passenger side for a moment, hesitating, having planned to take the pickup, but he finally climbed in. "We're going in style, I see," he said. However, as soon as they were on the road, Jerry remembered how much trouble Lyle had riding with anybody else.

His brother sat beside him chewing his nails, his legs braced. "There's a stop, Jerry. Yes, yes, yes. A stop. See it? You're coming to a stop sign. For Christ sakes, you're going to slow down, aren't you? We're coming to a stop sign. Don't miss the stop sign, now. That's a dangerous corner, you know. Yes, yes, yes," he said, when they paused, still not pacified, completely. "Did you see it? Did you see it, yourself? Honestly? Did you know it was coming up? It didn't *look* like you did. This is a dangerous corner. *Watch* it, now! It's a four-way stop, you know."

Lyle was not a pokey driver. In fact, he drove faster than the others, and automatically, talking all the time, but he thought of himself as being on familiar territory, forgetting they had all lived there once. "There's a fork coming up ahead, you know. You take a left at the fork. Go left. Yes, yes, yes! Left," he said, his feet still braced, his body against the door, as if ready to jump for it. "A left and then a sharp right. It's coming up *soon,* now, Jerry! Watch it!"

When he was back on the ground, he looked both sheepish and relieved. He knew, now, that he had not been reasonable, but he was willing to move on to other worries. The hardware store was crowded, and while Jerry waited in line with him, he unburdened himself. "Misty didn't come this year, you'll notice, Jerry. She's supposed to be traveling, in Europe, with her mother. They're in Europe, yes. So Charley says. He's drinking too much. Boy!" He shook his head, looking over the people in front of him. "Have you noticed?" Have you?" he asked. People turned, but he didn't notice. "Yes. Mother doesn't say anything. Little remarks, though, you know."

"Is Darwin coming up this year, Lyle?"

"Is Darwin coming up this year? Darwin? Supposed to, supposed to," he said, reflectively. He nodded. Then his expression changed. "Why? Why do you ask?"

"I'm just checking."

"Well, now that you ask, it's funny. Darwin didn't write home much this year, hardly at all. He *moved,* Jerry. Yes, yes, he moved, and for a while we didn't have any address. Does our mother look good to you? She doesn't, to me, no, sir, not these days. I tell her she's got to slow down some, at her age."

"You know how she is, Lyle."

"What'll I do in case she goes, Jerry?" (He never said "when.") Then his pale blue eyes lit up for a moment in glee, the kind of brief glee he showed sometimes over the absurdity of his limitations, a *brief* glee because his muted anxiety always caught up with him. "I don't want the place. I don't want the cottages. She wouldn't leave everything to me, would she? I don't want the responsibility. No, no, no. There's too much *work* for one person."

"You could sell, Lyle."

"Sell? Sell? Sell? The house and the cottages? *All* of them? You mean *sell* them? Sell everything? Do you? Is that what you mean?" His questions gave him a chance to think, to pull away, to work out the problem before he got back to people. "I suppose I could do that. Yes, yes, yes." He was at the counter by then, and he dropped the subject until they reached the street.

He took the next step. "She'll probably leave everything to all of us, though, right? Yes, yes, yes," he said, his eyes squinted, tearing a little with pleasure, thinking of their closeness. "All the brothers. We'll share everything, right?"

"We certainly would, in that case."

He finally located the real problem, and his expression changed again. What would happen to him if she died? Where would he go? What would he do? "Well, we don't want anything to happen to her, though, Jerry, do we?"

Jerry stood at the open window in the dark before bed. You could not hear the tide below until the house had settled like this—the children down, the adults ensconced in their various rooms. "Smell the air, Julia. Just smell it." He had grown up among the tidal reaches, the marshy smells, and the brackish, windy stretches, and when he was far inland, trying to make a living at this or that, trying to hustle up a dollar or two here and there, he sometimes wondered why he had drifted so far from the fundamentals. Oh, Longnook Beach and Ballston Beach, House Neck Head and Horse Leech Pond! "I haven't told Myra about our job problems, Julia."

"*I* never thought you would."

He turned. She was reading in bed, glasses pushed back on the broad, freckled forehead, Myra's small china soup bowl beside her, filled with cigarette ends. "I think Charley suspects. What if it gets to her?"

"Oh, you worry too much. She just hears what she *wants* to hear, anyway."

She was generally on edge these days, and because he felt defensive, he tried not to push issues. "I just don't see any point in burdening her with this."

"Well, that wasn't *my* point. If you want to worry so much, you could start worrying about money. As in the sense we don't have any."

He was furious. "What do you mean, Julia, I don't worry about money? I worry about money all the time!"

Darwin and Jason showed up the next day—Darwin just after lunch, Jason just before dinner, with his two boys. Given Jerry's three, there was a good deal of confusion. Everyone was in the kitchen while Myra was getting dinner. She stopped what she was doing every few minutes, trying to get the noise level down. "Hush, hush," she kept saying. "What happened to all the little ladies and gentlemen?" She opened doors, peered into closets. "What happened to all the little ladies and gentlemen? I don't see any little ladies and gentlemen around here!"

Jason went after Darwin, his little brother. "Heard we didn't know exactly what happened to you this winter, Dar. Mother for a while didn't have an address."

The criticism was still low key, but Jerry saw Darwin's jaw harden. "I was ill, for a while," he said, evading the issue.

Lyle was lifting lids, peering into pots and pans, ready to eat, worried about the time. "He looks fine now, Jason, right? He looks *fine!* He looks *good!*"

Jerry decided so. Darwin was pale blond, like Lyle, and he was cutting his hair short these days. It was straight, lying forward in a thick, stiff thatch. He looked as if he had started to work out again. He was in a sweat suit, and, if long past adolescence, he was, Jerry supposed, a "hunk." The term was Julia's.

"That's right, Lyle," Darwin said, obviously wanting the subject closed. "I'm fine now, just perfect."

Darwin was also queer. The world, Jerry decided, bulged with many curious facts, and among them all, he did not suppose that this curiosity ranked particularly high on the list, but if Darwin *was*—if he chased men—he was also his brother, his little brother, sharing the same blood: a mysterious entity, partly secure, a larger part not. "So, Jason?" Darwin said, "can we just *drop* the subject?"

Myra kept the two older girls moving, carrying the plates and the silverware into the dining room. "We all have our share of blessings, so tonight let's go around the table." She seldom carried out the threat. The idea, itself, was enough.

"Where's Misty, this year?" Jason asked, while Charley was wandering around somewhere with a fresh drink.

Myra was worried about the children. "These little pitchers have ears."

Jerry plunged in. "She's in Europe with her mother, taking her about. She couldn't go alone, of course, and Misty felt obligated. She's half-blind, you know, and she's getting up there."

"I realized they were having problems when they were here last summer, of course, but then, when I heard about their great loss, I hoped they'd pull each other over the rough spots. Have to, in a time like that."

Myra pursed her mouth. "I don't judge. I just never could."

Still in the crowded kitchen, sitting at the table or milling about, they heard a chair fall somewhere. Everybody assumed for a moment that Charley had gone down. However, the chair was in the dining room. The girls started blaming each other, and fighting broke out. Julia went in to check. "I may have to knock a few heads together," she said.

"Where *is* Charley, anyway?" Jason asked.

Myra turned. "Well, I mind my own business," she said, her tone strange.

Everybody waited, worried about what was coming next. But nothing did.

Jason finally cleared his throat. "We're all pretty grateful for what Mother's been able to accomplish alone over the years."

Jerry switched the subject. "What we want to know is how the painting's been coming along, Dar."

Darwin was standing at the sink picking at the wet lettuce with two fingers. "My God. Am I being interviewed? I just get depressed *thinking* about painting these days."

"Some of us have work to do, and they keep at it," Myra said. "They don't have time for depressions." She turned to Jerry. "I noticed that new car of yours."

Charley was standing at the door. He was mildly unfocused. "*What* new car?" he asked.

Jerry was going to try to raise some money, and he rose early the next morning. He wanted to get on the road before anyone was stirring, but Lyle was already down. He was making coffee. "Boston, Jerry? Boston? Boston, yes? You're going to Boston? *Now? Today?* Really? Boston? Why would anybody want to go to Boston?"

Jerry parked the Mercedes at Race Point and flew out. The morning was cloudless and already bright. He pushed back his recent failures. He felt firm and confident. He was an easterner, after all; he'd had two years at Harvard, and he was going into familiar surroundings, a man who had grown up around these accents and this aggressive pace.

He checked into a downtown hotel, showered and changed. He lowered the blinds against the sun, turned up the air conditioner and started phoning around, but he ended up talking to receptionists because half of Boston was out on a shore somewhere. He began to realize that he wasn't going to run into many well-heeled people still in town in the searing summer heat.

He finally had lunch with an old schoolmate who could not or would not help. He had dinner with a married couple on Beacon Hill. They had started to sell their silver, and he didn't mention his own problems. He spent the night in town, killing more time over a second lunch that did not pan out. He made a few more phone calls that turned into dead ends, and then he gave up. He took the six o'clock plane back.

He went uptairs while everyone was eating and opened his wife's jewelry chest. When Julia was on the road, she always carried everything she owned: costume stuff, largely, but, at the bottom, he found her great-grandmother's emerald brooch which had been reset in fragile-looking sterling.

He had the brooch in Provincetown before he realized he wasn't constructed for these kinds of errands, and he stood outside several antique shops before he could get himself to enter. When he put the brooch down on the velvet pads in front of these people, they pushed it around for a bit with the tips of their pencils before their expressions changed. They finally wouldn't touch it because the original setting had been replaced. They did not want it at any price, and they never got around to talking about money.

When he finally gave up, most of the shops were beginning to close on upper Commercial, and the crowds were thinning. He crossed the street and someone (a tourist) blew a horn at his back. The weather was shifting. It was blowing, clouding up, and for a minute he thought he smelled the wind from the outer shore. There was so much less booming on the bay, in the shifting kelp, the mild slush and weave, but while he was standing alone on Commercial, he sensed the open Atlantic. He shivered. And then, for the first time in his life, at forty-two, he began to understand that the world was generally uninterested in his survival. He didn't know why the fact left such an impression on him at the moment, but it did, and he was anxious to get back to his family. He wanted to be around his brothers.

It rained off and on during the night. Mist furled the shrub the next morning, and the drizzle moved in, a dense, enclosing world. Jerry didn't sleep well, and he was down early.

Lyle was making coffee in the kitchen alone. "Boston, Jerry?" he kept asking, in that troubled tone. "Boston? Did you really go to Boston? Boston? In that heat yesterday, too?

In that heat? All the way to Boston? Why would anybody go to Boston?"

Jerry was still under the previous evening's spell, that need to share his life with his brothers, and he broke under the questioning. He started talking without thinking about the consequences, and of course, the information just about crushed Lyle.

He was chiefly crushed because he couldn't help. "I don't *have* any money, Jerry," he kept saying. He finally rose and emptied his pockets. "Mother takes care of everything, and so I don't need money, do I? Yes, yes, yes. She takes care of everything." He finally ran into two dollars, some keys, some kitchen matches, some roofing nails and some loose change. Over Jerry's protests, he tried giving him the bills. "Mother buys the food. She pays the bills. *She* could help, though, Jerry! *She* has it! Yes, yes, yes! *She* has it!"

Jerry had trouble swearing him into secrecy. However, Lyle was so tactile. He understood touch before he understood anything else. Jerry put his hands on both his shoulders and held him until he finally calmed down. "All right, all right, Jerry! Then it's our secret. You can trust me, any day. Yes, yes, yes! You bet!"

Jason and Myra appeared. He was trying to talk her into going out to dinner that evening. "Take a night off, Mother. Why not? You've been doing all the cooking around here. What about some Chinese food? You like Chinese food."

She appeared to be considering the proposition, but at the same time, she had her removed look, suggesting that she was dealing with half-hidden pressures.

"Give in, Mother," Jerry said. "Let Jason make some reservations."

If she said, "Oh, I don't know," she meant she shouldn't. She wouldn't end up changing her mind, either. She would just decide she shouldn't, and the rest usually stayed unspoken. She wouldn't go, and without explaining why. On the other hand, if she said, "Oh, I don't know, I shouldn't," then the cat was out of the bag. She meant she would go if people could convince her to go. Once the family was onto the difference between the two phrases, they knew where they stood. Now she said, "Oh, I don't know."

Lyle resisted these distinctions. "Out to eat? Out to eat? All of us? Tonight? At a restaurant? You can go, Mother. Yes, yes, yes. You can go. Stop stalling."

"I just bought that nice, fresh cod. We all want that nice, fresh cod."

"It'll keep. Won't it keep?"

The children started to drift in, complaining about the weather. Still in their nightclothes, they lay across the furniture, waiting to be fed.

"Well? Won't it keep?"

Myra was stirring her coffee. "Oh, you ask too many questions!"

"Questions? Questions? Questions? What do you mean, I *ask too* many questions? What kind of statement is that? What's wrong with getting out of the house? What's wrong with a change? What's wrong with some fun? What's *wrong* with people wanting to forget their troubles?"

She put the top back on the sugar bowl and drew her mouth in a little. She looked at him and then at the children. "Little pitchers have big ears."

"Who's saying anything? *I'm not* saying anything." He turned to the room. "Am I saying anything, anybody?"

She knew what she knew. She played her cards close to her chest even when she did not have to, and because she did, it was hard to know just what she didn't know. "I just don't believe in rocking the boat," she said irrationally.

Darwin walked in. "What boat is that now, Mother?"

The sky cleared toward midnoon, and Jerry spent the afternoon on the beach with his family. While he was changing before dinner, he found three crumpled dollar bills nestled in among his clean socks, hastily seeded there in the upper right-hand bureau drawer. Then a five-dollar bill turned up in Julia's purse.

He had gone to Lyle rather than the others because Lyle's

love was the most durable, certainly the most unquestioning, but just because the love was unqualified, Lyle was killing him now. "I laid too much on him, Julia. I was stupid. I was unthinking."

She had just come out of the shower. She walked around in a towel, furiously combing her hair. "Oh, God! Lyle *could* grow up, a bit, if anyone ever *let* him! And if you worried as much about your *own* family, people wouldn't have to be hiding money around here, anyway! You wouldn't be going around begging in the streets!"

"I'm not begging in the streets!"

"You certainly aren't attacking the right people. Jason's got it. Charley's not broke, and Myra is *rolling* in it!"

"She *isn't* rolling in it, and in any case, at her age, I can't bother her with my troubles."

The argument accelerated, and Julia asked for a divorce. That wasn't uncommon. They each brought up the possibility from time to time, but the subject still cast a pall over them that evening.

Lyle wanted to grill the fish outside, his specialty, but Myra objected. "Do we want to fuss tonight? We don't want to fuss tonight, do we, if it's all the same to you."

"What's the fuss? I just wrap up the fish in some new potatoes, a few onions. Where's the fuss?"

She put some new potatoes on the stove instead. "Because it's just too much bother." She worried about a salad. Julia offered to put the salad together, but Myra said that she did not want help. She said that she was in charge, and that when she was in charge, she wanted to do everything herself. She worked on the vegetables while she worried about a nice dessert.

"We have ice cream," Julia said. "We have *tons* of it in there."

"We'll have ice cream and cake, then. I don't like to stint. I never could. I'll make a nice cake."

The family milled around the kitchen, in the way. Jerry needed a drink. "What's in the house, right now? What can we throw together?"

Jerry and Charley headed for the front parlor to look. The Coles rang the bell, wanting something or other, and Myra went in to get the door. The tenants refused to sit down; they said they had to get back, but they were both talkers, and they stayed to chat.

Jerry and Charley retreated, carrying the bottles back into the kitchen. "Dinner's probably going to be awhile," Jerry said.

Darwin was uninterested. "Just fix me a strong drink, and don't tell me about that."

Lyle was worried about the potatoes. He lifted the lid. "They're going to need more water. She didn't put in enough water. Should I put in some more water? What do you think?"

"*I'm* not thinking," Julia said.

"We've got rum, we've got whiskey. We've got a little gin," Jerry said. "What do you want, Julia? What about a pleasant evening?"

She looked at him without answering.

Charley scratched his head. "I'm *positive* there's more gin around somewhere, Jerry. *That* gin wouldn't help a midget through the night."

"Well, Julia said, "I suppose that depends upon how drunk the midget gets."

"Julia's right, Charley," Jason said. "Why wouldn't we all want to keep clear heads?"

Charley turned on him. "Nobody's *hiding* the gin around here, is he?"

"How melodramatic," Julia said, "for people not inclined to that."

"I wouldn't touch your gin," Jason said. "You just forget how much you drink."

"Julia! Jason!" Jerry said. "Listen, everybody! What's Mother drinking these days? She drinks rum, doesn't she? What about a decently strong Collins? I'm going to get her to *sit down* when she gets back."

Lyle watched him making the drink. He shook his head. "That's *too much* rum for her, Jerry, at her age. Yes, yes! Go easy on that rum, will you? You don't want to knock her out."

"Oh?" Julia said, but under her breath.

37

Jerry heard. He ignored that. "I just want to see her relax."

Charley fixed his martini in a tumbler, finishing off the gin. "Jerry's right. Let's get her to sit down, for once."

Lyle was watching the stove when Myra returned, and he started to fret as soon as he saw her. He was biting his nails. "Everything's going to burn! Don't they know when people eat? Don't they eat? For Christ sakes!"

Jerry was determined to change everybody's mood. He steered his mother over to the kitchen table and put the Collins down in front of her. "Everything's fine. Lyle's been watching the stove. So you *sit*. Tell us about yourself."

She sat. "I have too much to do," she said, but she picked up her drink. She sipped it tentatively. She put it back. She was deep in thought. "I'm coming along in years. I'm not always going to be able to cut the mustard, and when *that* day comes, I'm selling out. I'm going condo."

Lyle turned around at the stove. "That isn't for a long time yet. Why talk about it *now?* Why *brood* on it? You don't have to *dwell* on it, do you?"

"I want to get off this windy cliff. I want to get away from all this *sand*. I want to see some trees and some grass. I'm thinking about going back to Rhode Island. Why not?"

"You haven't tried the drink yet, Mother." Jerry said. "Try the drink."

She looked down at her glass as if tempted, but she did not touch it. She changed expressions. She tilted her head toward the left shoulder, poised in that meditative stance in which she meant to be most ruminative, most reflective—usually when she intended to spring some project. She cleared her throat. "Now, then. I've been meaning to do this. We're going around the room. I want to know the *one* memorable thing that has happened to him or her this year."

Jerry, Charley and Darwin exchanged glances. They needed time. Darwin looked at Lyle. He cleared his throat. "You go first."

Lyle looked at Myra for a moment. "Memorable? Memorable? Memorable? Here? You mean *here,* on the Cape? In *Truro?* Oh, no, no, no. Nothing memorable happens here," he said, getting up abruptly. He stood leaning over the back of his chair. "I've been worried about Jerry, though." He realized that he couldn't keep his secret any longer, and that made him angry. "Yes, I *am*, JERRY! NOW YOU LISTEN! I'M WORRIED ABOUT YOU! I always thought you were doing so *good* on the West Coast. Didn't you, Mother? Didn't you think he was doing good on the West Coast? Well, he lost his job. He lost his job, and he's been having a lot of money problems lately!"

Jerry's sense of relief took him by surprise, a swift, temporary sense of purification. Certain densities shifted in the upper chest, and for a moment he was breathing differently. He felt lighter. He looked around at his brothers, all his brothers. What did he expect? He expected concern. "I'm broke, all right." He smiled helplessly.

They felt betrayed and furious, as if, at any moment now, much more could come unraveled: their false starts and prevarications, their griefs, compromises and secrets. They could not blame Lyle, and all this intensity gathered around Jerry. Why, their eyes asked, would he tell Lyle such a thing in the first place? He could be such an idiot. Why couldn't they have a pleasant evening?

Myra came through, though. She was uncomfortable, and when she was, she got very firm. She set her mouth. She cocked her head slightly to the left. "What about the game?" she asked, in that tone. She broke the spell. "Jason? You're next."

Jason cleared his throat. He stood. He had obviously been preparing his story beforehand, and he spoke easily, without a break in the text. Jerry didn't actually catch a word of it, but he could feel his chest beginning to constrict again. He was back among them, breathing normally.

While Jerry and Julia were packing to leave, Jason called him downstairs. He hesitated for a moment, and when he saw that the coast was clear, he took him outside into the tackle shed. He finally pulled an envelope out of his pocket: cash contributions from Charley, Darwin and himself. Jerry steadied himself against what was coming next.

"This isn't much, a few hundred, Jerry, given as we could, but it may help. It may tide you over while you're trying to get on your feet. I suppose it's no secret that I can't understand what you do with your money when you have it. I suppose it's no secret that I don't understand why you appear to have so much trouble holding a job. Well, I wish I had some sound advice for you at the moment, but the fact is, I haven't. I don't pray often. We don't pray much, in this family, do we, but I'll pray for you," he said. He briefly touched Jerry's shoulder before he left the tackle shed.

Jerry went back upstairs to help Julia strap the luggage down. Julia took a shower. He was alone, stripping the bed when Myra knocked on the door. She took him downstairs, through the kitchen and back into her utility room. The huge washer was going, a relic, and she had to raise her voice over the noise. She grabbed his hand, opened his palm, and gave him two five-dollar bills. She folded his fingers over the money before she released his hand. Jerry could feel their crispness. She did not keep money around, and she must have gone to the bank recently. "Don't tell your brothers about this," she said, "because I can't do equally. I know I can't do everything about all the troubles around me, either." She looked off for a moment. Studying her face, seeing that faraway expression, he knew she was thinking about Charley's marriage: she knew about the separation.

When they left, Myra was sweeping the sand from the front walk. She is always battling the sand. She starts in the house and then works her way out to the porch, but the walk itself— the front and the side, going around to the back—always turns out to be the main challenge because it's so quickly buried. There is a covered patio behind the house, and when she has finished the walk, she starts on the patio. She has added both walk and patio in her own time, curious adjuncts up there in that open windswept edge of the world, but they offered her some sense of permanence. She sweeps the sand back into the scrub and the wild, knotty beach plum; she sweeps it back into the knee-high grasses and the half-hidden poison ivy. The light is just beginning to give. It is past mealtime, and the bulk of her day's work is done, but she sweeps on. Sweeps, sweeps, as Jerry's car disappears down the edge of the hill.

3 / Capturing the Magic

*J*ason Brewster flew to Boston on business in mid-March, and when he finished up there, he decided that he was going to drop in on his mother. He rented a car, drove down the shore route past Plymouth and swung onto the Cape around lunchtime. He ran into little or no traffic, always jammed during the tourist season. Most of the shops and motels were shut down, and for some reason this lack of action depressed him.

Lyle was there, getting ready to go out, but Myra was off shopping in Hyannis. If Lyle was both surprised and glad to see his brother, he seemed less effusive than usual. Changes, differences in routines usually bothered Lyle; people took their time going through explanations, then repeating them, in order to reassure him; but Jason's sudden appearance did not appear to affect him that much. His mind seemed elsewhere.

Jason was puzzled because Lyle was quieter than usual, and he asked him if everything was all right.

Lyle nodded while he was trying to find his car keys and then his coat. He was heading for a donut and pastry shop, and he asked Jason to come along. While they were getting in the truck, Lyle finally sensed Jason's concern. "I'm on a new tranquilizer, Jason. Yes, yes, a new pill. It's strong, and things just don't bother me so much. Makes me feel good. I'm fine, these days," he concluded.

Jason mentioned the deserted towns he had passed, all the way down Cape, the sparse traffic and the closed shops.

"You just have to know where to go," Lyle said. "You just have to know where to find the *life*. I know where the life is, yes. This place stays open all year."

Lyle always showed up while the merchandise was fresh from the oven, still warm and faintly soggy. Everybody in the place knew him. He went around choosing carefully, taking his time, sometimes changing his mind. "Smell the place," he said several times, nudging his brother. "Right? Right? The smell?" His eyes shone. "Stays open all year, too. Didn't I say it was open? Don't I know where to go?" He was putting on more weight, and while he chose, he rubbed his huge stomach. "Yes, yes, I know where the life is." He moved down the length of the counter, the clerk following with wax paper. While the clerk was winding string around the boxes, Lyle bought six elephant ears. They each ate one going back to the pickup.

Lyle wanted coffee. They stopped for coffee, and while he was ordering, he decided he was going to try the pie. He wanted Jason to try the pie, too. When Jason told him he was happy with his coffee, Lyle didn't press him, but his mood changed. He grew tense, and he stared into space. "Last winter, last winter, Jason, I had one of my little spells," he said. He stopped.

Jason waited while Lyle bent over his mug, stirring sugar into his coffee. Lyle had little spells from time to time. The brothers knew about these little spells in a general, if not a specific, sense. They never knew details. Myra did not believe in dwelling on the subject. Jason cleared his throat. He knew that Myra would not appreciate Lyle's going into detail now. "What happened, Lyle? Do you want to talk?"

Lyle looked up at Jason, his pale blue eyes paler than usual, and misty. He shook his head. "I put our mother through a lot of trouble, Jason. Yes, you know, a lot of trouble. She *helped* me a lot, Jason, yes."

"She can be strong, Lyle."

They were sitting in the window across from each other in the empty coffee shop. Jason's brother told his story while he looked out onto the deserted street. While he talked, no traffic passed. When she sent him on an errand into Provincetown last January, he drove the pickup out to the Boston airport instead. He loved watching planes, but while he was there, he forgot where he was, or who he was, but nobody paid any attention while it was still light. The police got curious after dark. They got into his wallet, and called Myra. Lyle stirred now, without taking his eyes from the window. A wind had sprung up, blowing sand from the bay across Route 6A.

Lyle stretched his long legs under the table. The table rim cut into his huge gut. He reached into his back pocket for his wallet, and he stood. He paid at the counter, helping himself to a toothpick, and Jason followed him out. Lyle looked confused for a moment, but finally climbed into the pickup. He put his keys in the ignition without starting the truck yet. "Why, Jason?" he asked. "Why? What *happens* to me, at those times?"

Jason shook his head. "You'd need an expert to tell you that."

Lyle started the engine. He talked, some, on the way back. This and that. He was briefly hospitalized. When he emerged, he was on a different tranquilizer. He still "saw" someone in Hyannis, but as far as Jason could tell, his doctor on these trips merely renewed his prescription.

Jason decided that Lyle needed counseling, but given Myra's views on the matter, Jason could not push it himself. She couldn't understand why anyone would want to tell all his personal business to a perfect stranger. She was closemouthed and independent. She never let up on herself, and she expected from her children that same kind of reserve. "When you think *you* have problems," she was fond of telling them, "just consider the *real* problems in this world."

Her childhood was a case in point. Her mother died when Myra was barely sixteen, leaving her to run the house and to raise two younger sisters. Her father, Jason's grandfather, had been a reserved, formal person, always correctly attired, and though a laborer, he had been thought of as an old-fashioned gentleman. He talked little and smiled less. He generally kept his thoughts to himself, but when angry, he could express himself.

When a long hot spell moved into Rhode Island once, she set up a card table on the side porch, ready for the evening meal, including napkins and napkin rings; but he was too deeply dependent upon his daily routines—certainly above eating in sight of the street—and when he discovered her girlish preparations, all the blood left his face. He picked up the table, broke its four legs, and tossed it over the porch rail into the lilac bush.

She didn't dwell on the past, of course. She said that she preferred to look ahead, and she always accompanied that remark with a good deal of cheerfulness. However, a certain wry assertiveness turned up in curious places. She had hung throughout her rentals typed little mottos or sayings: warnings, hints, instructions, as if she dealt with rowdy elements, when, in fact, the same, solid, upper-middle class couples returned to the same cottages year after year.

> Welcome to this little home
> We hope you treat it as your own
>
> If you smash or break a dish
> We hope you replace it is our wish

Jason noted a growing inwardness through the years. She seemed confused at times, as if hidden anxiousness put her at cross-purposes. When that happened, she cocked her head to the left and narrowed her eyes, looking for action, another project.

Jason arrived that summer in rough weather. Melodramatic-looking masses of black cloud rolled in from the Atlantic. The blurry hill looked barren, the cottages huddled in the slanting wet, the grasses beaten back, the sandy stretches pockmarked. Behind a rental, sodden wash was twisted around the clothesline, and a child's oversized Star Wars beach towel, hanging too low, was snarled in a broad, thorny bush.

The rain let up shortly after dark, then returned during the early morning, falling steadily and softly, the wind gone. Cooped up, lying across the furniture on their stomachs, and staring at the floor, the children looked fretful, frazzled. Jerry's two girls, at that age, were ready to start something at any minute.

Julia collected them after breakfast. She was taking them to town just to get them out of people's hair. Jerry decided to go. He was working again, ready to spend some money.

Lyle shook his head over the weather. "It's been like this for days. Yes, yes, yes. It's been like this for days, and I can't get out. I can't get any *work* done. I've got a lot of work to do, right? Yes, I have. Yes, yes, yes."

Charley was fixing a drink. He was never far from a drink these days. He carried his gin upstairs and put it on the sink when he showered, and when he stepped out, he reached for the gin before he reached for the towel.

"I can't get any work done. How am I going to get any work done? Tell me that."

Darwin was straddling a chair, his chin resting on the back. Hunched that way, he was considering Lyle. "Why not just take it easy, then? What can you do about it? What's the point in not?"

Darwin did not always take into account what he said, and he sometimes tried to treat his brother like an adult. Jason loved Lyle as much as Darwin did, or ever could, and he could not see much sense in the remark.

Lyle looked up, instantly troubled. "Take it easy? Take it easy?" He stood there in the middle of the kitchen, shaking his head. He looked at Darwin, trying to puzzle that out, and then he looked over at Jason. He was trying to get some answers out of them, but as usual, he finally had to work through the problem himself. "You mean don't worry about not working? Don't worry about not getting anything done? Is that what you mean? Yes? Is that what you're saying? Why worry about it? How am I *not* going to worry!" he concluded, the idea finally too farfetched.

Myra had bread in the oven. She was washing out mixing bowls. "That's easily said," she observed, without turning.

Father Bandom dropped in with his troubles, a big man in his early sixties. He had a shock of bushy white hair, bushy white eyebrows. "I have these three vacationing priests on my hands. You know how cramped I am, Mrs. B.," he intoned, lowering himself into a chair. "I can't pack three strapping boys into those two spare back bedrooms. I need my study, of course, and so they can't have that. They wouldn't want that, would they? Why would these mere boys want to stay with an old man, anyway? Wouldn't they feel as if they're being watched?"

Myra seldom took people from the street, but the Donaldson family had canceled at the last minute. "I think I could just squeeze in a week."

The priest lit a cigarette, looking for an ashtray. He dropped his match into a cup. He rubbed his palms together. "Wonderful, wonderful, Mrs. B. I knew I could count on you in a pinch. They're coming all the way up from New Jersey, and it's this spot I had in mind. Right on the water as you are. Good boys, too. Wet behind the ears, a bit, but I hear from fine homes. Fine, fine homes."

Lyle was back at it. When he picked a subject, he was going to explore the possibilities. He sat across from the priest, shaking his head, talking to the room in general. "I hope it clears soon," he said, cracking his knuckles one-by-one. "I *like* to keep busy. It's *good* to keep busy, right?"

The priest finished his cigarette. He hesitated a moment and then put it out in the cup. "Keeping busy doesn't accomplish everything, does it? When we keep too busy, we sometimes keep from confronting ourselves. We avoid our true natures." He leaned back in his chair and turned his head toward the oven. "What's that divine smell, Mrs. B? Fresh bread? Don't I smell fresh bread?"

Lyle's eyes widened. "Keeping busy? Keeping busy? Keeping busy is *bad?*" He glanced around at the others in appeal, wanting his security back. "Keeping busy is bad? No, no, no," he insisted, distraught. "I *need* to keep busy."

Myra's face was flushed. "Oh, I don't *believe* in all that Freudian *stuff!*" she observed, as if dismissing the occult.

The priest look amused. "What 'Freudian stuff,' in particular, Mrs. B.?"

"I just don't believe in all that *stuff!* I don't believe in the unconscious."

He was caught off-balance with delight. "Oh, that is marvelous. Marvelous. And in the middle of the modern age, too. A bit like not believing the world is round, isn't it?"

Darwin was getting interested. He looked at Myra, amused. "Why *don't* you believe in the unconscious, then?" he asked, pleased with the absurdity.

She turned on him. "Oh!" she said, upset, "you're *filled* with such bitterness. Why are you filled with such bitterness?"

The accuracy of the remark took Jason by surprise. He never knew what she knew and didn't, and at the same time, the untypical directness threw him off-balance, as if he were witnessing something he wasn't supposed to see. He felt vaguely soiled, responsible. "What if we drop the subject, Darwin?"

Lyle couldn't. "Why? *Who* said the world isn't round? It's round, isn't it? Yes, yes, yes, it's round."

The priest rose. "Well, Mrs. B., I certainly thank you, and I enjoyed our little conversation." He put up his blunt, bluish-white hands, palms exposed. "I'll let myself out. Don't bother! Don't bother about me! I'll send the boys along."

The oven timer went off at that minute. Myra turned, startled. "Oh, all this *talk*. All this *fuss,* and look what's happened! I almost forgot my bed in the oven."

The next day broke pale and clear. Lyle was down first, then Myra, and when Jason showed up, the coffee was on. Lyle was out in the tackle shed looking for his toolbox. Myra was getting the cottage ready for the three priests.

"Well," Julia said, looking out, "they're at it already, aren't they? The two of them, like little beavers. And happy again."

When around while they worked, Jason felt disconnected, scattered, at loose ends. "Things pile up, Julia."

He watched the family getting ready for the beach after

breakfast, gathering lotions, blankets and beach toys. Jerry picked up the folded playpen stuffed with spare diapers. Stairs creaking, doors slamming, and then Myra came up the hill carrying soiled linen.

Jason held the door. "How can I help, Mother?"

When he asked what he could do, she always said the same thing. "You can help," she said, saying it now, "by staying out of the way."

He decided to join the others, where he could feel less visible. He followed the trail behind the tackle shed, heading for the stairs that led to the bay. The space over the water was already hot, white and still.

They were huddled together on the sand, engaged in conversation, looking up toward the house every once in a while, as if worried about being overheard even from that distance. He knew they were discussing her.

"I love that priest," Charley was saying. "Didn't you love that priest?"

"That was such a wonderful slip, that one about the bed," Darwin said.

Jason sat down, feeling as if he were betraying his mother.

Julia lit a cigarette. "Well, if you ask me, it was pure justice."

Jason burned silently. He couldn't see it—and educated people, being amused at her expense. What was the point?

Charley looked at Darwin. "I thought that remark she made about your bitterness was curious."

"*What* bitterness?" Darwin asked, miffed.

Julia put her cigarette out in the sand, her right cheek partly shaded under the straw brim. "Oh, you're *all* bitter. Let's face it."

Jason decided he was going to stay patient. "She's had her hands full, you know, through the years, Julia. She's actually done wonders," he said, and they all turned, dutifully registering his presence, but said nothing. "Raising us, I mean."

The drift and spume. The children ran along the shore's edge, in and out. The tide was up, coming toward them in long, gentle, rolling swells.

Jason decided to change the subject. "Did you ever consider trying to paint some of this, Dar?"

"Oh, God! *Look* at the people who *have.*"

"They're not all bad, then?"

"I'm not into landscapes, Jason."

"Still, I'm surprised you don't get inspired. Just trying to capture the magic."

Darwin rolled over on his side. He rubbed his stomach under his T-shirt. He studied the group for a moment, without saying anything, and when he spoke he changed the subject. "I feel as if I'm on hold up here, with everybody. But maybe I don't even resent it, people pretending I don't lead the life I do."

Jason tensed. Why bring that up, the homosexuality? "What's wrong with some diplomacy?"

Charley was amused. "Why? What about your life?" he asked. He was certainly not that opaque.

Lyle suddenly appeared high above them. He was hammering on a cottage roof. They could hear him over the children's shouts, the gulls' racket, the easy slide of the water.

"Lyle changed his prescription again," Jerry said, pleased, Jason decided, with the inside information. "Evidently last spring he had one of his little spells."

Jason was taken by surprise. He thought that had been confidential. "Seems perfectly fine now, to me."

Darwin pulled off his T-shirt and stretched out on his stomach. "Why? What happened?"

"Apparently he took the pickup and disappeared. Wound up in Boston."

"Why isn't he seeing a real therapist?" Darwin asked, knowing.

At that point they saw Myra leaving the priests' cottage, now in shape, carrying cleaning equipment. She stopped off at the Coles' place. While she was on her rounds, she paused to chat here and there among the rentals, checking on their guests, feeling out the particularly interesting ones for special attention. She looked for summer talent: a musician, an actor, a poet. She took advantage of their gifts. She organized, getting people together. She'd had a violin solo on the patio several years back.

Jerry was staring at the water. He pushed his sunglasses down from his forehead, where the skin was beginning to peel. "From time to time Julia and I have talked about having him out, with us, for a visit. Doesn't he ever need some sort of change? Wouldn't the world close in on anybody here?"

"In which case," Julia said, "the magic is in the eye of the beholder."

"What magic, Julia?" Jerry asked, still involved with his own ideas. "Haven't we said he ought to come out?"

Jason had asked his brother to visit him several times, just for the same reason, the change. "Yes, yes, yes," he'd say, working on the idea, "Chicago? Chicago? Chicago? Fly out? Yes? Visit you? Visit you in Chicago? I might do that." Then he'd glance at his mother while considering the whole project, waiting for her to object. She wouldn't, not directly, but he would wait, wanting her to, ready to seize on the objection. "Well, why not? Why *can't* I see some of the country? Wouldn't it do me some good?" However, he worried about being away from familiar surroundings, and he never went. People dropped the subject.

The children were still occupied. The older ones looked for shells, the younger interested in discarded bottles, bits of broken styrofoam. They filled their buckets, then turned the treasures over in the sand, just out of the sea's reach for the moment; when they went back for them, they were gone.

Darwin still lay on his stomach, running sand through his fingers, his feet crossed at the ankles. "Having him visit has crossed everybody's mind."

Jason looked down at the broad young span of his back. "In an efficiency, Dar—you don't have much room there, do you?"

Darwin rolled over on his side. "Oh, come off it, Jason. What do you think's going to happen to him with me? Just through osmosis he turns queer?"

Jason was shocked. He had never heard him use the word before. "Now *wait* a minute! Wait right there! I didn't say—"

"You don't have to, do you?"

Everybody was silent. Nobody seemed to know where to look.

Julia reached for the cigarettes beside Jerry. "Oh, all this *talk!* All this, as Myra says, *fuss.* *None* of you is about to bother having him visit and you know it. Nobody's taking the bull by the horns."

The priests turned up shortly after two o'clock. They appeared in shorts, and they did not stop to unpack. In shorts, without shirts, they looked fit, fairly nondescript. They spent the afternoon throwing a ball back and forth among themselves in the open, weedy lot behind Myra's house. She passed the window every once in a while. She was already calling them her "boys."

Father Bandom returned. (Behind his back, Charley called him Father Bedlam.) Stamping his feet on the sill, shedding sand. Stoops. Bends. Picks a cocklebur from his trouser leg. "I've just stopped by to see if those boys have been behaving."

Jason let him in. If he didn't, the priest would keep him standing there at the door.

The family did not attend church much. However, Charley was an active athiest.

"We haven't had to call the pope yet, Father."

"Oh, no, now, don't be bothering that holy man. Don't be giving him more paperwork." He followed Jason into the front parlor, where they were having an after-dinner drink. "What's that? What's that? Would that be brandy? This is a civilized house, a civilized house!"

Jason gave up. He poured him a brandy. "They stick together, Father. They don't go far. They've been throwing a ball around all afternoon."

He sniffed the brandy before he touched it. "Yes. Well. Now. You know. Free from Jersey, and you let those types smell a little salt air. Probably goes to their heads. Gives them high spirits. Good to get out of their tight collars. *If* they wear them these days, which I doubt. But you know these modern boys. Give them a guitar, and they think they have a service going. I don't interfere! I don't interfere!"

There was a lot more of this before Jason cut him off. "Do you want to see them? They're back there now."

He shook his head. Standing there sipping his brandy, slapping his pockets, looking for cigarettes. "No, no! Don't bother! Don't bother yourselves!"

Despite the shower, Jason felt drained after the day on the beach. The brandy merely increased the effect. The warm breezes were up, blowing curtains, banging shades and rocking a loose door back and forth upstairs: constant movement, a world in flux. The light was dying in the big bay window.

The priest managed to get his cigarette lit. "I'm fairly new around this area myself—or 'new' as the natives would call me. You can be here for ten years, like me, and as far as they're concerned, you're still just visiting. But put here to make do, and without the proper help. The church is falling apart. I can't get carpenters out. Nobody wants to work. You call, somebody says 'Wednesday,' but *which* Wednesday? You never know."

Myra kept a curious collection on the bay-window sill, a random assemblage of objects she had picked up on the beach over the years, nothing unique: clamshells and seaglass, periwinkles and starfish, some smooth white stones and a few pieces of driftwood, not arranged in any particular fashion, not arranged at all, in fact, but there, where she dropped things when she entered the house. She had also placed up there a leg with a claw foot which once fell from a chair; the chair was gone, but the leg remained, a part of this dusty, if permanent hoard.

Father Bandom was still searching for an ashtray. He finally settled on a clamshell from the collection. He looked burdened, given his drink, his cigarettes and his shell, but Jason did not ask him to sit down. He was afraid he would never leave.

"So. What with one thing or another, I'm kept hopping. No rest for the weary, even on a beautiful spot like this. Somebody has to take care of the tourists. When the summer season hits, what with the added heads, I don't get a free moment. I shouldn't be complaining, though, I know. I'm not stationed in New Jersey yet, am I?"

Myra and Lyle entered the room, just in and on their way

back out. Lyle was carrying a plunger. When Myra reached the door, she took the clamshell from the priest's hand and put it back on the sill. "Everything in its place," she said, sounding distracted, disconnected. She opened the door. She was gone.

In the silence that followed, the movement upstairs seemed magnified: the door banged, the shades creaked, blown back and forth. Lyle flushed over his mother's behavior.

Had the priest noticed? He wanted to know if Lyle ever did any handiwork for others. "Some light carpentry," he said. "You know. Just some patching up."

Myra opened the door. She stood there impatiently, waiting for Lyle. He was still flushed, put out. "Wait a *minute,* will you, Mother! I'm still talking. Can't you see? For God sakes!"

The priest put down the brandy and raised both hands. "No, now I've got to be going. I just thought, Lyle, I'd put that idea in your head."

Lyle paced around the kitchen after breakfast. "Should I? Should I? What does everybody think? I'd have to drive down there every day, wouldn't I? Wouldn't I? That's a long trip. It'll take up my time," he said, as if arguing with his mother against going.

She looked at Jason. "He'll go or he won't. In the meantime I have to put up with this. I wish that priest had never entered this house."

Her objections worked on Lyle like a stimulant. "But I've *got* the time, don't I? Don't I? Yes, yes, yes, I've got it!"

Jason wanted to be helpful. "You won't be overextending yourself, will you, Lyle?"

"Doing too much? Doing too much? Is that what you mean, Jason? Doing too much? I like to keep busy. Ma? You know that."

"I don't know anything," she said. "Keep me out."

"I've got to get my prescription filled, anyway. I have to do *that,* don't I? Don't I? Won't that get me out from underfoot?" He paused, waiting for that thought to sink in. "While I'm going in that direction, I'll just see what he wants done. No harm in *just checking*," he said, looking for the car keys. "I'll be back for lunch."

She shook her head. "I'm saying nothing," she said.

Lyle did not show up for lunch. Considerably put out, but refusing to discuss the matter, Myra threw the meal together in silence, as if she were furious with the whole family.

Jason paced, looking out every once in a while. He was remembering the Boston problem.

Lyle was on everybody's mind. "That's a good drive, round trip," Julia said. "What's the point in fretting yet?"

Jason was less sure. "How has he been these days, Mother?"

"When he thinks he has problems, I remind him of the world's problems. I know I have a few."

Lyle turned up after three o'clock. He headed for the refrigerator looking for the ice cream. "I can do it! I can do it! No problem there, no problem. It's *easy* work! Anybody could do it. Jason, *you* could do it," he said, a little joke. He walked around the kitchen spooning the ice cream directly from the carton. "Ma? What do you think?"

She was coming out of the utility room. She was boiling, just boiling. "I'm saying nothing," she said, "not a word."

He stood in front of her with the ice cream. Huge, towering over the little woman. "Ma? It would be a change for me, wouldn't it? It would get me out of the house, from under your feet." Then he was wondering if he could handle the change. "I don't like to get that reputation, though." He shook his head. "If I take on that job, then everybody thinks I've got time to work for them. I can't be running all over, can I? I can't afford the reputation!"

"Well, if you started the job, you've got to finish it. I certainly know I would."

He opened the bread box, looking for donuts. "*Start* it? I *told* you. I didn't start it. I just went down to see what he wanted done. I didn't have my *tools* with me, even."

"Then what have you been *doing* all day? What takes that long to do in a priest's house?"

54

He rolled his eyes at her while he was chewing on a donut. "We talked, some, yes."

"*Talked?*" she asked, "talked?" as if that would have been the *last* idea in *her* head. "What did you talk *about?*"

"What do you mean, what did we talk *about?* We just talked. We had lunch, for Christ sakes, and we saw part of a ball game. Where's the Cokes? Didn't you buy any more Cokes?"

"Did *you* remember to go to Hyannis?"

"*Hyannis?*" He smacked the side of his head. "My pills! Right? You mean my pills? I forgot my pills? Yes, I did, I *completely* forgot my pills! Jesus Christ! I'm getting forgetful these days, right? I can't remember a *thing!*" he said, as if intrigued with his limitations.

Myra was spending more and more time with the priests. In appearance, they appeared to be in their twenties; they were in their middle thirties: clean-cut, clean-shaven, trim, urban, in chic, open sport shirts, gold chains. New Jersey middle-class, mobile, hard, third-generation Italians.

Julia saw her disappearing down the hill, carrying a clam pie. "And I thought she had this anti-Catholic thing."

"Oh, no," Jerry said, "just that priest. Who got off on the wrong foot."

"Which foot was that?" Darwin asked, wanting to get something going.

Lyle was spending more and more time at the church. "*You* know which foot," Jason said.

Jerry wanted to settle things down. "Listen, both of you, I vote for a pleasant evening."

"Who gets to vote?" Darwin asked. "Who said this is a democracy here?"

Myra wasn't generally what she called "social." She said that she did not have time for such pleasures. However, before the season ended, she tried to have the rentals up for a picnic on the patio. Everybody brought a covered dish. When the spirit moved her, she started organizing. She decided that, this year, she was going to have a folk mass first.

She had the Protestant's fascination with rite, a world beyond hers which was both more lavish and more austere. She had been raised a Lutheran (though never a steady churchgoer), but she didn't make fine distinctions among the various liturgical branches, and the young priests, as performers, now struck her as fair game.

"Everybody can use the uplift," she said. "I know I could."

She spent that day getting the house shipshape, just in case anyone walked in. She planned to confine everybody to the patio, just to save the house, and she worried about the weather. That morning was clear, the afternoon pale, colorless and gummy. She reminded everyone that the patio was covered, anyway. "Even if it rains," she observed, "people will enjoy the open air."

It began to drizzle an hour before the event. Charley and Darwin left for Provincetown. They claimed that the evening was too arcane for them, and Julia raised her brows. "Too which? Ducking out is what they're doing." Lyle was down at Father Bandom's, but due back at any minute.

The priests arrived first. They milled around self-consciously in their rayon shirts, white ducks, smoking cigarettes. The guests filed up in separate groups with covered dishes, carrying sweaters against the chill. The wind shifted once, slanting the drizzle into the patio, and people changed positions. The priests distributed their mimeographed materials. Myra showed up last, wondering where Lyle was. They started without him.

The service was brief, clean linen on a card table, the temporary altar: many light touches, some introductions and instructions, readings, a five-minute homily, two songs. The clergy passed the peace. When one of the young men shook Jason's hand, his fingers just touching Jason's, he looked over his shoulder at the same time, eyes dulled by the routine. Then the bread. The cup was not shared, and Myra was unpacking the paper plates twenty minutes later.

The children darted around the food, in and out among the guests, waiting to be fed. The wives uncovered the dishes. The drizzle turned into thin rain, just visible against the lighted house. Because of the damp, people stood, holding the paper plates. The priests kept to themselves, smoking again, flinging the cigarettes out of the patio into the shadowy compound.

When the young men finally had their plates filled, they hurriedly crossed themselves in preparation. Then they stood together in silence, without utensils.

Myra hurried over. "Eat, eat," she said. Then she saw the problem. She went off to find utensils. To save herself work, she used plastic forks, spoons, tiny plastic knives. Big men, their size in contrast emphasized midget cutlery.

She took Jason aside by the arm, gripping him just below the elbow. Once she had people together, she always wondered why she had bothered in the first place. She was also worried about Lyle. "Call that church, will you? See what's going on."

Jason went inside without telling the others. He closed the parlor door behind him before he called. He got the housekeeper, who was talky. She had not seen Lyle and did not know where he was. She extolled his many virtues before Jason could finally stop her. He asked her where the priest was. "Why, he's on a call," she said. "Isn't he always? Yes, I'm *sure* that's what he told me. He's on a call."

Jason told Myra. "Did he ever pick up his pills?"

She set her mouth and put her head to one side. She wanted to get rid of everybody as soon as she could. "We want to keep everything looking normal," she said. "Just act normal."

The bad weather was on her side, and people drifted off early. The priests left first. Hugging themselves in their thin sweaters, the women began to gather up their bowls.

Jason and Jerry stacked the chairs, carried in the last of the trash. Nobody mentioned Lyle.

Myra stayed out there alone, getting things shipshape, pulling and tugging at the benches and the picnic table until everything had its former empty look.

She was still out there when Darwin and Charley turned up drunk, talking loudly. Charley made fresh drinks.

Jason told them that Lyle was missing, but he had trouble getting through. "Well," he said, "trust you two, in an emergency, to be in this state."

"Oh, *come off* it, Jason!" Darwin said. "Come off it, Saint Leviticus, will you?"

Julia had just finished putting the children to bed. She looked drawn, severe. "She's still out there, in the rain. While you boys are having at each other."

Jerry was standing in the doorway. "Lyle should be seeing a shrink. That's the point, and not just somebody pushing pills. What if we *could* get him to visit one of us, away from her, Charley? What about your therapist?"

"Who presses his coming?" Julia said, her voice flat and tired sounding. "Who's really tried? What makes you think anyone's going to try now? Truth is, you all struck an unspoken deal years ago, and you know it. Just to stay unencumbered. Free and clear. They get to have each other."

Jerry shouted at her. Jason wasn't listening. He was looking out the window. His mother stood there for a moment in the patio, in the emptiness. Then she turned out the light.

Lyle walked in with his buddy, the priest. They had gone bowling, then stopped for a few beers. He disappeared, on his way to the bathroom.

Myra showed up, blinking against the sudden light. "I don't know what you want, or what you're up to, Father, but we're a close family, and if we have our little problems, like other families, we keep them to ourselves. We don't seek outside help." Five feet four, she drew herself up straight. "*Physician*," she concluded, a little too stridently, "heal thyself!"

He flushed. He looked flummoxed. He started to raise his hands. He looked as if he were wondering if he was dealing with a loose nut. "Oh, well, then! Well, now—anything I can do! Just anything. Don't hesitate." He let himself out.

Nobody spoke at first. Jason heard the car start, then turn in the drive. He cleared his throat. He looked at Jerry, avoiding Myra's eyes. "What's so wrong with Lyle seeing someone, Mother?"

Jerry nodded. He looked at Charley. "We could chip in, all of us, if it's the expense."

"I'm perfectly willing," Jason said. "We all need some help from time to time."

"Oh, the professionals!" Myra said. "The professionals! Just *don't* get on that subject again. Just *don't start!*" She had turned white. "I just don't want to hear about it!"

Lyle showed up. "I know what you're talking about. Yes, yes, yes, I know. I know, all right. I'll tell you what I need to keep in mind, if I can speak up for myself. Mother needs me. She's getting old, and she needs me." He looked at Myra, as if she were going to object, and if so, he was going to cut her short. She didn't. "Yes, you do. You know you do. You can't manage by yourself. So don't answer back."

Jason wanted to return to the original subject. "You've got to think of yourself first sometimes, Lyle. We all have to from time to time. There's no crime in that."

Lyle turned on the room, the whole pack. "Nobody's *listening!* LISTEN TO ME, WILL YOU? WILL EVERYBODY? For once? For *Christ sakes!* I'm *trying* to tell you I'm all right when I remind myself she needs me. I can stay on course, then, Ma? Yes, yes, yes!"

Myra turned away. She walked into the kitchen, and Lyle followed her out. The room could hear them back in the kitchen together, arguing about something else.

Jerry looked at Julia. "Well? What else did we expect?"

"You're all free and clear," she said.

Jason was still standing at the window, his back to them, looking out at the empty patio. They belonged to each other, his mother and his brother, and so cemented, their bond kept everyone else at a certain distance. He felt abandoned. And unsubstantial, unsolid, standing in his own skin, peering out.

4 / Parker's Visit

*W*hen Jerry drove up his mother's hill that summer, he passed a familiar sight: a tourist's car stuck in the sand, spinning its wheels, getting deeper, on its way to China. The mother and three children helplessly clustered beside the small Ford, looking hot and disheveled. These people usually turn to the cottages around in desperation, ready to call a garage, where they get soaked. The local garages assume that they deserve what they get, and Jerry couldn't keep up with the going rate.

His brother rescued them from time to time, and Lyle was crossing the field in his pickup at the moment, chains rattling in back. He never took any money. When people tried to insist, he would just keep shaking his head, backing up to escape the proffered bills. "If I was in your shoes," he would explain, an utter impossibility, "wouldn't I want help?" He turned angry when he had trouble communicating, and as big as he was, people soon dropped the subject.

Myra would sometimes argue with him. "It just encourages more traffic," she'd point out, as if these people would soon spread the good news, until mired cars cluttered the landscape in all directions, but since she long ago discovered that he was going to do what he was going to do, she usually saved her breath.

Aside from her rentals, the hill wasn't a tourist spot, and since she had the same guests every year, these people weren't tourists in the usual sense. The beach flow was residential, re-stricted. The residents wandered down from the cliff taking jerry-built stairs. Keep Out signs cropped up everywhere.

When Jerry pulled in, Myra was standing on the porch close to the ship's bell that belonged to Jerry's father, the captain, a flagpole on the other side. She was looking past the whale's jawbone covered with morning glories, staring into space. She had her head to the side, in that meditative stance in which she shut the world out. Alone with herself, processing infor-mation. A short, stocky little woman with fleshy arms, sturdy legs. "I have news," she said as soon as the car doors opened. No greetings. No small talk. Just that: "news." She might have seen them an hour ago. "Oh, yes, and you, too, children. You're old enough now to enjoy this." She still stood there treasuring her secret and the attention.

Jerry's family scrambled out, climbing over each other's various parts, deliberately. The girls fought off and on crossing the final stretch of interstate, but had fallen asleep coming down the coast. Now refreshened, the energy level was high. Jerry's boy, just past four, never stopped. He headed for the giant jawbone.

"Children!" Julia shouted. "Now! Your grandmother's speaking!"

Myra wavered, uncertain; a second idea had come through, jammed against the first. "No, no, no," she explained impa-tiently, correcting Julia as though she never listened, "that's all right, that's all right. We'll wait until everybody's at the table tonight. Doesn't everybody want to hear this?"

Jerry unstrapped the luggage from the top of the car and car-ried it into the front hall. Darwin was on the phone in the par-lor. He had the door closed. He was leaning against it, and Jerry could not shove past.

When he finally hung up, the phone instantly rang. Jason had been trying to get through from the airport.

"Who's handy?" Darwin asked through the open door. "Who's picking Jason up?"

Jerry drove, Darwin beside him deep in thought, hands clasped between his big knees.

Given the weekend, the highway was cluttered: people checking into cottages, others checking out, pulling boats and trailers, the family bikes strapped in front. The cars weaved in and out. Jerry commented on the flux.

Darwin had his head down, staring at his knees. He shrugged. "Well, the Cape's composed of glacial drift." He seemed preoccupied. "New York's hotter than hell right now, and Parker's air conditioner has broken down."

"Who's Parker?"

Darwin looked out for a moment. Then he glanced at Jerry, briefly. "Oh, Parker's Parker."

Jerry didn't actually know much about his little brother. He wondered if he wanted to talk about the phone call, but he didn't ask. He did not want to pry.

They had one of those rare, perfect Cape days: the ocean side a ruler-straight line of blue, flat and bright; the pale dunes separated that plain from the second blue, the brash cobalt sky that turned up in every art gallery from Provincetown to Hyannis.

Jerry swung off the highway into the shadowy, cooler woody sections that sheltered hiking trails and picnic spots. They climbed until the foliage gradually thinned; the scrub returned, and they were back in piercing light. The car passed hitchhikers on the way to Herring Cove. They turned when they heard the car: four tall, gaunt, feisty-looking young gays.

Darwin was watching them. "My God, what's happening? We've spent years, we've spent our lives, painfully learning that it's okay to be sensitive, it's okay to have feelings, and what roles do they choose now?" he asked, switching pronouns. "With all that black leather, those army crew cuts? With their bushy sideburns and emaciated chests? Why, they all look like hoods. Why do you suppose they all want to look just like hoods?"

Darwin told his brothers something about himself from time to time, one brother or another (if not when they were together), as if his need to share himself occasionally overtook his usually cautious nature. He was quiet again, after his question, as if he were waiting for a response. Was he? Jerry never knew, but he knew that if his response wasn't just right, he could lose him in a minute.

"It's an unconscious parody, perhaps?"

Darwin leaned forward, as if he were hard of hearing. "Of *what?*"

"A macho role, Dar?"

Darwin sat back. He looked at Jerry, bemused, and then he smiled, as if such arcane subject matter were bound to be over Jerry's head. "You don't know *what* you're talking about," he said.

Jason's ex-wife had taken the children west that summer, but if he was alone, he was still mysteriously upbeat. "A wonderful flight, a wonderful flight," he kept saying on the way back to the car. "Perfect weather, too. Perfect weather."

He stood beside Jerry while he opened the trunk. "Did Mother tell you anything?" He searched their faces, waiting. "Anything?" They didn't know what he was talking about. "Well, I've done it. I'm engaged."

They shook hands for the second time. They patted him on the back. They fussed over him while they were climbing into the car. Jason sat in the rear, but he leaned forward to talk, his arm on the edge of the seat directly behind Darwin's back. "Listen. I don't think I'm supposed to say anything, just yet. Mother may want to, and I may have spoken out of turn. It's her announcement, so let's wait. You know she'll need the center of attention tonight."

The light held through five o'clock, like high noon, and the crowded kitchen was airless. The children milled, fretful after the beach, and despite earlier intentions, Myra fed them first to get them out of the way.

"Children should be seen, but not heard," she said.

Julia raised her brows behind her back. "What makes her think she wants to see them, either?"

Lyle pushed cartons around in the bread box, looking for something to tide him over.

Myra was cutting up cabbage. "I don't know why you can't wait, like the rest of us. I don't know why. I have never understood."

He found the donuts. "That's the *point,* Ma! You don't get the point!" He looked around at everyone, tearing with pleasure, his little eyes screwed up. He loved having everybody around. "I have to eat while I'm *waiting,* don't I?" He was putting on more weight. "How else can I wait?"

Jason came down. He had dressed for dinner despite the weather. "When does Charley get in, anyway?"

Lyle opened a Coke. "Charley? Charley? Charley? You mean Charley? When is he getting in? *Ma? When's Charley getting in?*" She was back in the dining room at the moment, taking the children their dessert, and when she answered—something short, sharp, as if she didn't want to pursue the subject—they couldn't hear from the kitchen. "Tomorrow, Jason," Lyle said, evidently knowing. "That's tomorrow, right? Yes, yes, yes. Some time tomorrow. Ma? *Right?*"

Given the special occasion, Jason had bought an expensive wine. He wandered around looking for wineglasses. "This is an important night."

Lyle was impressed. "Wine? You bought wine? Jason? Wine?" He stood there biting his nails. "Shall I have some of that? I think I'll have some of that." He smacked the side of his head. "Jesus! What's happening to me? I almost forgot! That's right! It's a big night, isn't it? Yes, yes! You're engaged. I'll *definitely* try the wine, tonight."

Myra came through. Jason turned. "I can't find more than four wineglasses, Mother."

"I'll just have a juice glass. I don't mind."

"You need a new set. I'll have to remember that."

"Wine is wine. We don't put on the dog very often in this house. I know I can't, with my bills."

Lyle was at the table first. He tried the wine while people were still milling.

Myra stopped him. "You're forgetting the toast," she said, under her breath.

"The toast? The toast? What toast? Oh, yes, yes! Toast!"

She tapped on the side of her juice glass with her spoon, her head to one side. "I have an announcement." She paused, waiting for everyone's attention. "Some big news, some answered prayers. Charley and Misty are back together. Those two lovebirds have made up."

Jerry was skeptical, at least. She usually believed what she wanted to believe. She wanted to hold onto her children's marriages as long as she could, a natural reaction. If Charley and his wife had been separated ever since the miscarriage, Mother treated the separation as just another lovers' quarrel. She didn't let him talk about his troubles, either. "You two could work it out if you tried," she said, more than once. "You just have to try. You should *both* come down to earth," she would conclude, a favorite phrase when she wanted a subject dropped.

Jason cleared his throat. "Well, if it's true, it's wonderful news, of course. I don't deny that."

Jerry suddenly remembered Jason's announcement at the airport. "Isn't there more news, Mother?"

She looked puzzled.

"Oh, yes," Darwin said.

Lyle half raised himself from his chair, coming close to upsetting his wine. "He's *right!* Jerry's right! Yes, yes, yes. Mother? You didn't tell ALL THE NEWS!"

She paused, and then, when her eyes caught Jason's, she remembered.

Jerry hadn't told his wife yet. "What's going on, anyway?" Julia asked.

"It isn't all that crucial, Julia," Jason said.

"Oh, shit, Jason," Darwin said, embarrassed for him.

But Lyle was still shouting over them. "WELL? WELL? WHAT ABOUT IT? WHAT ABOUT IT, MA? WHAT ABOUT JASON? HE'S GETTING MARRIED, ISN'T HE?"

"Just engaged, right now," Jason said.

Lyle's shouting finally unnerved Myra, and she snapped at him. "All right, all right! So I *forgot!* I'm getting *old,* aren't I, and I forget. That's all. I forgot!"

Lyle rolled his eyes. "Oh, *Jesus,* Ma, don't talk like *that!* Don't start *that* again, please!" He glanced around, looking for support. "She just forgot, didn't she? Why is that such a big deal?"

Jerry slept late the next morning, and when he finally reached the kitchen, he found Julia and Jason sitting over coffee together. She was trying to draw him out.

"Mother can show some favoritism, of course," he was saying, working on the problem. "That's a fact. But why dwell on it?" he asked, in that bland, neutral tone. "How long are we up here? Why not keep things pleasant?" He seemed to want to pursue that subject for a while before he brought up the main business. "Curious, too, because I never thought I'd marry again. Too busy, I told myself. Tax law doesn't allow much time for a social life. Besides, you know, once burned, and I was, pretty bad. But that's also water under the bridge."

The family was scattered around the place. Jason appeared to appreciate both the quiet moment and the undivided attention. He was usually reticent, hidden as he was behind his dead-earnest convictions, but from his standpoint, he was baring his soul and he was, in his way, fairly touching.

"I've known Suzanne for some time, actually, and we'll both admit the courtship wasn't always easy going. People our ages, you know, can get pretty set. Habits and such, but that's natural. She's really a wonderful human, all around, and I've learned a lot from her, in fact. She's been trying to bring me out of myself."

Jerry poured himself some coffee. He couldn't walk out, but at the same time, he couldn't get himself to sit down; it was too trapping. He stood leaning against the sink half-listening to a good deal more of this stuff. He was thinking about Myra, a complicated woman. If she had favorites, she switched them from time to time just to keep the world hopping.

There was suddenly a lot of commotion in front of the house. Jason paused in the middle of a monologue, agitated because interrupted. Charley appeared first. He had put on weight. Even his face was filled out, giving him a kind of puffy, genial expression that hardly fit the showy, cynical temperament. "What's going on back here? Why is everybody in seclusion, like monks? Why does everybody look half-dead?"

Misty showed up next. She was from the middle of the country, a softer culture, in many ways, and she was still unused to this blunt eastern approach, a frontal attack which can mask some goodwill. She raised her brows. "I'll never understand him, Julia, not in a hundred years." The two women hugged each other briefly.

Charley found a Coke. He had stopped drinking, and he kept a Coke near throughout that vacation. He stayed close to Misty, always within touching distance, as if this physical arrangement were a constant, necessary sign of reassurance. "Well, we're reconciled," he said. He was ready to discuss his marriage, though still making wild swings around central issues. "This thaw is a renewal. Springlike. A wonder. A miracle. The world's a mysterious place."

Misty was wearing her baggy white jump suit—overpopular by then, seen everywhere, but if a cliché, Jerry decided she freshened it. She looked elegant. Brown and lean. "Miracles? I don't know much about miracles. We're just trying to work things out." Once a trusting, exuberant child, she had turned into a quiet woman with reservations.

Jason was washing the coffee cups at the sink and stacking them in the rack. He was alone in his corner of the room. All these chores his, of course. "Well, that makes sense," he said. If self-exiled, he wanted to be noticed.

Jerry was amused. "Jason's engaged."

Charley was putting ice in his Coke. "Really? *Jason*, Jerry?" He finally looked at Jason. "How long has this been going on? Who is she?"

Jason cleared his throat and wiped his hands on his mother's dish towel. "Well, actually, you know, it's a long story."

Charley poured his Coke. "I'm not drinking any more. I'm off the stuff, completely. Right, Misty?"

"He's really been trying."

"I've been doing more than trying," he said, still pleased with the encouragement. "I'm not even myself these days. I feel very light, very airy, very spiritual, not drinking, as if I'm composed of cloudy stuff." Misty turned. "Where are you going?"

She reached for her purse on the table behind her. "Where am I going? I'm not going anywhere."

He put his arm around her, drawing her back into the circle. "I never knew that drinking made me feel so *cohesive,* but without it, I feel as if *parts* are about to fly off in different directions." He paused. "I'm not criticizing. I love you, Misty."

"I love you, too."

They appeared to live within the limits of these self-imposed strictures, and if the arrangement kept them fairly occupied, it must have drained other resources.

Myra appeared, her arms filled with shopping. Jerry wondered just how oblique she was going to be, and she did not fail him. "All right, who's in college now?" she asked, first off, without context. She put her bags down on the table. "Is anybody here going to college?"

She was proud of her sons' educations. She enjoyed counting the degrees they collected through the years. She paused now, and when her eyes got that narrow, squinty look, Jerry knew she was counting. "Now, let's just see," she said, using her fingers, beginning with Jason. "You went to Boston U first, right, before you switched?"

She usually left Charley until last. They were all college bred (excluding Lyle, of course), but Charley had three degrees. She called his Ph.D. "the big one."

Charley broke in now before she could reach him. *"Mother! Misty's back!"*

"Well? So? Why is that such a surprise? Who was right in the first place? Who told you two lovebirds to come back down to earth?"

Myra intended eating on the patio early, but she did not get organized early, and Lyle got a late start out there with the fish. The family milled around with drinks through this period, at odds and ends, feeling in the way, wanting to help.

Charley picked at the potato salad. "If you can't wait," she said, "at least get a dish. I didn't bring you up to eat out of the bowl like that."

"It won't taste the same." But he got a bowl down from the shelf, spooning the salad on his way into the other room. He sat down beside Misty, who had a drink. "Here we are, I with food, you with your Manhattan."

"Is it bothering you too much?"

"I didn't ask you to stop drinking just because I have stopped drinking."

Jason passed, at loose ends. "You're really putting on the weight, though, Charley."

Charley didn't hear him. He was playing with Misty's bracelet. "I never really noticed how *narrow* your wrists are, like little bird bones." Everything about his wife that summer struck him as totally engrossing.

Jason cornered Darwin. He brought his drink over to the window seat where his brother was perched, and he pulled up a rocking chair. "I didn't invite Suzanne up this year because I wanted to feel out the ground first. She's divorced, and she has a child. When I casually told Mother about this, she didn't answer. When she doesn't, she doesn't approve. She doesn't have to say anything."

Darwin was waiting for a long-distance phone call, and he was preoccupied. He kept checking his watch.

Jason looked up at Jerry. He wasn't sure if Darwin had heard him or not. "She has a very precocious son, younger than my two. The boy needs a strong male figure around, in fact."

Darwin stirred. "You've been divorced yourself, Jason. Jerry's been divorced—twice."

"Is it because she's a woman? Is that the difference? She's always harder on women, isn't she? Different standards."

"She'll finally accept what she has to accept."

"Suzanne's her own woman, too, I'll admit. Independent, with her own interests, and she'll pretty much say what *she* thinks."

Darwin looked amused. "*Whose* reservations are we talking about?"

Jason hovered between irritation and curiosity. "Reservations?" He was finally interested in the attention, and as an attorney, he was ready to explore the subject disinterestedly, in his usually careful if circular fashion. "Do you suppose I have some, at this late date?"

The phone rang. Darwin jumped up. "I'll get it! I'll get it!"

They could not clearly hear the conversation behind the closed door, but Darwin's tone was unmistakable: sometimes pleading, sometimes biting, bitter, intimate, often patronizing.

Jason rocked. He suddenly glanced down at his feet. He got up, pushed the chair back, straightened the rug. He was looking for problems: breaches, rents, tears, loose ends. "Why do you suppose he lets people call him here, at the house?"

Jerry's earlier goodwill evaporated. "*What* people?"

"Don't be obtuse. Don't calls like that just raise questions that don't have to *be* raised?"

Myra appeared. "All right, I could use some help. Some strong men. Chop chop."

While they carried out the chairs, she set the picnic table, trying to hold the paper tablecloth down in the sudden breeze from the bay. "You know, as I grow older, as I reach this plane of existence, I often wonder what it's all been about. You're educated people, and you're supposed to know. Simplify. Am I right?"

Lyle was on his haunches in front of the grill, checking the fish. "Mother's talking about retirement." He did not this time carry on about it.

"I bought a cottage down in Wellfleet, and I'm getting it moved up here as soon as the foundation's in. I hired a bulldozer, but Lyle's finishing the cellar himself. I'm going to retire, and I'm going to move into it. I'm going condo with the other cottages. I'm going condo with them, and then, this old house? I'm going to *sell* this *old* barn!"

Lyle peeled the foil away from the main course: steaming cod covered with parsley, small onions, tiny, buttery potatoes. "That's not now. You aren't going to retire now. She makes it sound as if it's soon."

"Soon is soon. We all know what's coming. I know I do."

The screen door slammed. Darwin came out carrying the beer and the wine. He passed Charley. "And you aren't drinking," he said reflectively, as if he were still mulling over the fact.

"I still feel a little unreal. I'm not used to this otherworldly plane."

Misty came from upper-middle class conservative Catholics, where the standard virtues are taken for granted. "Oh, *Charley! Why* always carry on about it?"

"Everybody's going to be pleasant," Myra said.

Charley looked at his family. "Was I carrying on? Was that my point?"

"How about just dropping it, please?" Misty asked.

"Everybody's just going to come back down to earth. What should I be reading these days, Charley?" Myra asked him, the Ph.D. "Can you recommend something current? *Good* books, now, not fiction."

"Everybody's home," Lyle said. "Yes, yes, yes. Everybody's together again."

"I know I should sit down with a good book now and then, but I can't concentrate when I know something important needs doing."

Julia appeared, carrying the children's sweaters. They were running back and forth outside the compound in the dark, occasionally flashing past. They appeared inside the patio now and then, around the potato chips. "They'll stay out there in that wind until you *force* something on them," Julia said. "Why don't they notice temperatures, like people?"

Darwin was still thinking about his phone call. "New York's still boiling. Parker, I think, is coming a little unglued."

Lyle was still on his haunches in front of the grill. "Parker?"

"He's in a state."

"Oh, yes," Myra said, "those painters, those artists, right?"

"Parker doesn't paint."

"Am I correct, though? A lot of temperament. You must meet all kinds of interesting people down there in New York, the art capital of the world. I know I wish I could."

"Do you?" Darwin asked, interested. "Well, we could get him out of the city heat."

Lyle stood. "Parker? Is he a friend? A friend of yours, yes? You're thinking about having a friend of yours up here? Up here? To visit? Someone you know from New York?" Any outsider worried him. Would a visitor upset his routine? Would he fit? And how would *he* be, himself, as host? What was expected? "In this house, here, this summer? Do we have room?"

Myra, Jerry noted, did not exactly put a damper on it, yet. "We're hardly in the talking stage."

Lyle considered the hestitation a rejection. "*Sure* there's room, Ma! There's room. There's room. Isn't there always room for my brothers' friends?"

"Yes, and Parker's always appreciative," Darwin said.

"We've pretty much limited these summers to the family, haven't we?" Jason asked. "Trying to make contact among ourselves. Trying to catch up. Surely this is important." Darwin didn't answer. Nobody spoke.

Lyle brought the platter to the table. "All right, get your plates, everybody! Come and get it! Nobody's going to go hungry here! Where's the children?"

They had waited so long they were ragged, overextended. They did not do much more than pick at the fish, pushing the garnish aside. Jerry's youngest refused to touch it.

"Everybody's here! Everybody's home! The whole family! Aren't you glad you came, kids? Everybody's together!"

He cracked up some wooden crates, and the flames slanted through the splintered pine, throwing sparks. The family settled on the benches in the wind, just comfortable in sweaters, knees turned in, elbows almost touching. They passed the salads and the chilled, cheap white wine in styrofoam cups.

Myra half rose. "I know what's missing. A prayer! We have to have a prayer! Freeze in place, everybody!"

They were caught. She was waiting, and they knew they were going to have to go through with it. They bowed their heads, avoiding each other's eyes. The doxology followed—a weak, faintly keening sound just below the wind's racket. The shadows moved across the ceiling above the glowing coals, the hissing, snapping pine. While they were still in the middle of this Christian duty, they shared a common self-consciousness, an unease that brought them together, and when they raised their heads after the orotund hypocrisy, the fragile spell still lingered. The small talk was mild, colorless, without bite or sting.

Charley was telling Julia about his former marriage problems. Jerry was there, but Charley spoke directly to her. Like most men, he needed the woman as a focal point when he discussed relationships. "If you saw her parents' house, you'd think you knew the type—a lot of floral wallpaper, china cabinets, collections of Dickens' fictional characters in porcelain, that stuff, but you actually wouldn't. You'd be wrong, Julia. When Misty's father was alive, the parents camped and climbed mountains together. When he dislocated his shoulder on a ledge somewhere, she got him down and back to camp, ten miles away. They weren't close, though, but according to Misty, they never fought, never exchanged a cross word. Too formal for that. Catholics, they just endured. He died shortly after I met Misty. Do you know what I think he died of? Bottled rage. Why am I telling all this?"

A young family crossed the field behind Myra's place. Coming down the winding, narrow back road, the illicit traffic soon reached a dead end, and when the tourists emerged, they soon realized they weren't going to get any closer to the water below. The small, stocky, untanned child ran ahead toward the stairs. The mother called, pointing to the Keep Out sign. The child stopped, objecting, but stood where she was. Tall and unfleshy, both in designer jeans, the man in large rimless glasses, the two stood there shoulder to shoulder, holding hands, entranced with the view. Given both the dusty, silvery-grayish moors above and the distance down, a steep drop, the blueness that stretched in every direction shimmered like a hallucination against the pale, fawn-colored sand.

"I was away when Misty had her miscarriage, with a lot of fighting before that. I was at a conference, and so, you see, she felt abandoned. She went back and forth about the miscarriage, blaming me, blaming herself, blaming both. I realized then she kept a lot hidden. She wouldn't listen to reason. The parents' strong, stubborn streak manifested itself, without having its roots in dogma, and before I knew it, she was packing, pulling out. I still don't think that Misty would have left me if she didn't have her mother to run to—the source of all that will—but while she was there, she had a kind of breakdown. A lot of Catholic shrinks and priests. I didn't learn that until much later. The breakdown, I guess, cleared the air."

The tourist family left the top of the stairs. The woman took the child's hand, and the three crossed the field together, back to the car, defeated. Then the neat trick. A driver must make a U-turn in the narrow lane with no shoulders, but if he isn't careful, the back tires slip into the sand. Jerry watched, holding his breath. The man seemed aware of the problem, and he turned cautiously, just making it. The car disappeared down the hill.

Jason suddenly materialized. "What do you people make of that conversation the other night?"

Charley frowned, with more story to tell. "*What* conversation?"

"Mother doesn't know about Darwin's tastes, does she? How could she? Coming from the generation she does."

Jerry didn't particularly want to pursue the topic. "We could be worrying for nothing. What if his friend could pass? Darwin passes."

"Do you think so?" Julia said. "It may be hard to say, since I know. But I think I would know."

Jerry was annoyed. "Just *how* do you think you would know?"

"Just the body language. There's something about his too-perfect bearing."

Charley looked vexed, too. "His too-perfect *what?*"

"He watches himself too carefully."

"You're able to spot them anywhere, right? Julia's gift."

Jerry tried to keep his temper.

"All right, Charley, take it easy."

"*I'm* very fond of your brother, myself," Julia said, "*if* I'm permitted."

"So let's drop the subject, Julia."

"Well, I'm all for dropping it. Who brought it up?"

Jason stood there frowning, still worried about the main issue, his mother. "Who is he, anyway? Does anybody know?"

"He's from Jamaica."

Everybody looked at Julia. "How do you know?"

"How else? I asked. Parker's a student. He works nights in a cafeteria, where Darwin met him. Darwin's looking after Parker, sort of."

"Well," Jason said, "what now?"

Charley was amused. "Then we also have a racial issue, Jason."

"I'm just wondering how much mother wants to swallow."

"We could put him up in Wellfleet," Charley said, "and with nobody the wiser. Mother's got that cottage there. Take food down after dark."

"I don't know why that's funny," Jason said. "I fail to see why. The problem is, we're not getting anywhere."

"I can't see her cooped up in a two-bedroom cottage, anyway," Julia remarked, thinking about the retirement plans. "I thought she was eventually going back to Rhode Island. Isn't heaven supposed to be there?"

"Perhaps that's the point. Rhode Island's a mythical place."

Lyle wanted to show everyone the incomplete excavation. The family could see it from the kitchen window—if not the hole itself, then the damp, sandy loam lying around it in low piles, waiting to be trucked out. Small white butterflies, moth-size, hovered over the uprooted bayberry.

Julia moved the curtain a bit, trying to show interest. "It looks very impressive."

Lyle was getting into his flannel shirt. "You can't see it from here. What can you see from here? What can you tell? I'm taking everybody down there."

Myra was getting her cleaning materials out. "His treat, too. Who can go gallivanting all over today, though? I know I can't."

Everybody was scattered. It was going to take some time to round up people, explain, probably argue, then head them in the right direction. Lyle himself could get waylaid. Julia wanted to start, if they were going, but Lyle expected them to wait. He wanted everyone together.

Myra wanted to get at the kitchen floor, and they were in the way. Caught between conflicting wants, Jerry felt a primitive sense of paralysis, a drifting sensation of shapelessness.

"Come on," Julia said, feeling no pull, "I'm starting."

Since the early morning overcast, the space had exploded, opened up in all directions. High on the rise, a slight breeze blew across the stubby crests, stirring the poverty grass, but the metallic blue below was motionless, unwrinkled. The cellar had been dug where this view was best.

Julia paused without leaving the trail, worrying about the poison ivy. "Is this what we're supposed to be admiring? It's a hole, all right, isn't it?"

The back door opened. Myra appeared, then Charley and his wife. Myra cupped her hands over her mouth. "Here come the two lovebirds, everybody! Make way!" The two started down the trail toward Jerry and Julia, single file. A cat followed unhurriedly, keeping its distance, half-interested, but still part of the parade.

"I wasn't surprised when they got back together, Jerry," Julia said.

Charley stopped to wait, where the trail briefly widened, and he took her hand. She was wearing flimsy runner's shorts and a V-neck cotton shirt. She was a part of the eighties, given this bloom and fitness. She was hipless and ribby, long-limbed. They paused there, as if not ready to join anyone yet. She had her hair up, and he brushed the back of her bare neck with his open palm.

They seemed isolated from the family that summer—when they argued and when they made up. They seemed to talk around or over people. They stayed encased in closeness, in discussions the family could not follow or did not particularly want to overhear. Such intimacy was at least disconcerting, often embarrassing, and although the family tried to go on doing what it was doing, this intimacy and tension were finally distracting. Around them Jerry felt shadowy and peripheral.

Waiting for Lyle, Darwin appeared on the back stoop. He leaned his coffee mug on the rail while he talked to Myra. His blond hair had gotten lighter in the sun. It was straight, longer than the previous summer. Like Misty, he looked as if he could be doing health commercials.

Then Lyle appeared with the children, the whole crew. Evidently everybody was taking the tour. He had brought out an old float, left in one of the cottages, and while he was trying to blow it up, the children crowded around. Myra was keeping someone's baby for the day, a child from the second cottage on the left, down toward the water. She had given it over to Jerry's daughter for safekeeping. Jerry's second oldest girl, from his second marriage, was eleven. She was carrying the baby now. ("Oh, God," Julia commented, "I told her to put him down. Do you suppose they woke him up?") Jerry's daughter was small for eleven, slightly built, still clumsy. The grip was makeshift, and the baby dangled in front of her uncomfortably. Darwin took over. The baby was exchanged, and he started down the hill toward the hole. He had the baby against his big chest, supporting both neck and bottom. Jason appeared last, following Darwin.

Julia did not want to presume. She cut across the field to relieve Darwin, but when she reached his side, he evidently did not object. She stood there talking while he still had the child firmly ensconced against his chest.

What was she saying? Her straightforward nature worried Jerry from time to time. He headed across the openness toward their crest in a warm, disarming wind.

However, Julia did not want to encroach. She had evidently been trying to pick her way around the possible brambles while staying supportive. "Well, if you want to have him up, then have him up. Isn't it your business?"

Jason shook his head. "It just isn't that simple, Julia."

"Ignore Jason."

Darwin looked at Julia skeptically. "Really?" The bundled infant slept, dead weight against Darwin.

"Yes, really. If you like him, wouldn't we?" Nobody used the word *gay*.

"Parker's a bit rough around the edges, but he can be very engaging."

Darwin had a propensity for picking up people who turned out to be beneath him, and Jerry wondered (too readily) if he was now having second thoughts. "You're safe, anyway. Your life will still be your own, Darwin."

"What do you mean, Jerry?"

"Oh, that's easy," Julia said. "You know your mother. She only sees what she wants to see. The rest goes right over her head."

"But I don't *want* him to go over her head. I want to share him. Is my sexuality removable from who I am? Is yours? Jason's engaged, and he brings wine. Misty shows up, and everybody's happy. Why is she not supposed to know who I am? She's my mother, Julia."

What was actually going on inside him at that moment? Jerry went numb, starting with the fingertips, spreading to the wrists. There are some needs, some needs, that appear to lie undisturbed within, safely quiescent for most of peoples' lives, given the pain they cause; but when they finally surface, they appear to break through a thin membrane.

Julia, too, realized how unbalanced he was that summer. "Oh! *Darwin!* You *won't* get through! You *can't!* You'll only hurt yourself!"

Darwin flushed. "Why take that for granted?" When nobody answered, the silence dismissed the question. And then, when some common sense returned, the color left his face.

Jason rescued them. Unashamed, still perfectly opaque, he took charge, missing the point. "Look, buddy, I'm *not* old-fashioned," he began, clouding the painful with his clichés. "I know, in its place, you have the right to your own life. I'll be the first to defend it."

Darwin looked at each in turn. "This is a family delegation, isn't it?" His voice was terribly low, hardly heard. There was some comfort in the misunderstanding. He shrugged when Jerry protested. He handed the infant back to Julia. "It doesn't matter. It really doesn't matter. I shouldn't have come up this year in the first place. Who knows what Parker's up to? I shouldn't have left him alone down there."

Jason watched him go. "Well, I took the heat, didn't I? Still, if someone has to take the heat, I may as well take the heat. Here I stand. Generally, I'm considered to be the thick-skinned family member, anyway."

Myra spent the day cleaning the kitchen. She had several interruptions, first from tenants wanting this and that. Then a couple appeared wanting a cabin at the last minute. She didn't have anything available, but she showed them around the grounds. A fit-looking pair in their middle sixties. Considering the featherweight oxfords, chino skirt and rugby shorts, Charley called them the "L. L. Bean people." They caught her interest.

At the time when she was usually fixing the evening meal, she was still organizing the spice shelf. She had everything down on the counter. People wandered in and out. She finally noticed. "I have an announcement to make, just in case you're at all interested. I haven't started supper yet. I haven't started to *think* food yet." Jerry offered to take them out, but she refused. "It's too much fuss," she said. "It's too much bother."

Julia offered to help, but Myra seemed too disconnected to know what she wanted done. "I know I should have had something started by now, but I'm not an *organized* person, Julia, and I'll say it myself. Take heed, everybody! Take this lesson down! Make lists!"

Charley was downing Cokes. There were times when he felt more ravaged than most, and certainly these times centered around the dinner hour. He followed Jerry into the parlor, at loose ends. He needed a drink, but short of that, he needed Misty around. She was in the shower. "Do you know what Myra's done now? Guess. Just guess!"

Jerry couldn't.

"She's *already* rented that cottage for next year! The retirement cottage, still down in Wellfleet on jacks!"

Lyle came down. Jerry's brother after his shower—shaved, hair slicked back behind his large, glossy ears. Wearing a drugstore shaving lotion. "Do you know what she's done now?"

"Charley just told me, Lyle."

"Did he? Did he? Really? Did you, yes? You told Jerry?"

"He knows, Lyle."

"About the retirement cottage?" His eyes welled with delight, considering the absurdity. "She's already *rented* it! Get that? Do you? Do you? How she was going to retire early? And she's already *rented* it!"

He made few concessions to the heat, but because he was off work, he was in plaid Bermuda shorts that dropped below the huge knees. Tight across the expansive bottom, the thick, meaty thighs. "When's supper? When do we eat? Where's Darwin? I haven't seen him all day."

Myra was in the door. "He had to go back to New York."

"New York? New York? Where he lives? Are you sure? Why?"

"Business came up."

"What about his friend? Wasn't he having a friend here?"

She leaned forward, her head to the side. Then she looked around, back toward the kitchen where the children were. "Little pitchers have big ears," she observed, and then Jerry knew she knew. She had known about Darwin's homosexuality all along. "Well, I can't stand here. I've got *people* to feed! Everybody just come back down to earth!"

Myra was going shopping, and on the spur of the moment she decided to turn the trip into a family outing. She called the children.

"They've been in the sun all day," Julia said. "They're strung out."

"Oh, they'll be fine. They'll behave. They'll behave with me. I don't get to see the grandchildren that much, the short time they're here, and they'll enjoy the change."

Julia wasn't unpleased. She wanted a nap. "It's going to be a tight fit."

"We'll all fit. We're family. Come on, everybody! We're going to see the sights."

Jerry drove. Charley and Jason sat in front, Misty, Myra and the children in back. Myra passed out gum, collecting the wrappings and putting them in her purse. "This is an outing, isn't it, children? We're having an outing. We're going to see the sights. We're going to keep our eyes open. But we're going to sit still, aren't we? Nobody wants to be crushed."

When on an excursion, she usually headed for Orleans or Hyannis. She went down to these places just to get away when she was by herself, spending the better part of the day taking in the shops, but they were just going into the Provincetown A&P to pick up some necessities. When Jerry reached 6A, he hesitated. He wanted to know if she planned taking the scenic route or the short trip down 6. She chose 6 because she said she had supper to fix.

The children started to quarrel among themselves as soon as Jerry swung onto 6. Since they spent so much time on interstates getting to the Cape, they balked as soon as they spotted anything resembling a highway. "We're all going to be pleasant," Myra said firmly. "We're all going to be little ladies and gentlemen. We're all going to enjoy ourselves, aren't we? I know I am. I know I don't want to be crushed."

Misty was trying to tell Myra about their place in Iowa, the farmhouse on several acres. She was sanding and stripping wood. "Oh, I wish you could see what I've been doing," she said. She started to explain.

Myra still had her mind on the children. "You're not looking, and you're not taking advantage, people. Aren't we out to see the sights?"

Beside Jerry, Charley squirmed, feeling separated from his wife. He turned around every once in a while to check the back. "She was restoring the place when our early problems hit. Steaming off wallpaper, stripping trim, pulling drywall down."

Misty waited until she thought he was through. "I'm on that small front hall now."

He wasn't. "When she left, I lived in the middle of these grand ruins. I stepped over disconnected circuits, loose plumbing, unsafe floors." He paused, admiring his metaphor.

They passed some bikers, strung out and sweaty, loaded down with packs.

Myra leaned forward. "Oh, look! Look! You're going to miss the tourists. Don't they look interesting? Aren't they having a good time? Don't you wish that when you're older, you can go on a bike trip like that?"

Jerry pulled into the A&P parking area. An immigrant family came through the doors, inland crop pickers who seldom showed up this far out. The large, darkish mother was wearing a clean cotton house dress, white cotton socks and men's work shoes. She appeared to be in charge. The group (the mother, the smaller man, the four children) clustered around while she passed out postcards. They did not have any packages. They had evidently gone into the store just to buy the cards. They spent a long time passing the cards back and forth.

The children wanted to go in with their grandmother, and when they discovered they were not, they set up a commotion in the back.

Myra eased out alone, leaving instructions. "I'll just be a minute. I'm picking up some basics. Watch the scenery and report. There's a lot of interesting things to see. Just *look* at those interesting people," she added, spotting the crop pickers. "I bet you haven't seen interesting people like that before. Don't we need all sorts?"

Charley, like Jerry, did not smoke around Myra. He lit a cigarette behind her back. It was his usual drinking hour, and he had trouble sitting still. He looked at Jason. "So. Why don't you tell me about yourself? Who put Darwin on the plane yesterday? You?"

"We had a fruitful discussion first. We cleared the air."

"*Fruitful?* I love it! Everybody's queer these days, Jason. Everybody's queer these days, and you're going to have to adjust. My mailman in Iowa is queer. Did you know that? A rural mailman who comes around in a fairly jaunty little jeep. Very butch-looking, very brusque. He has a small, stylish moustache, and he lifts weights. The United States Post Office accepts him, and if the United States Post Office can help these boys to come out of the closet, then you're certainly going to have to adjust."

Jason had been looking out the window, as if not giving full attention to this speech. "I know you assume that's all very amusing," he finally said.

"I don't know why it's so funny, either," Misty said, from the back. "I know you *think* it's funny, but I don't see why it's so funny."

Charley turned around. "Why? What's wrong, Misty? Why are you so upset?"

"I'm not upset." Her voice was low, so neutral, so matter-of-fact that Jerry wasn't prepared for the rest. "I'm not upset. I'm enraged. I feel enraged most of the time, too. *Many* women feel enraged most of the time, Charley. They just don't show it."

Jason cleared his throat. Nobody spoke.

Myra returned. "Well, what have I missed? Have I missed much? Has anybody seen any more interesting sights?"

They were pulling into the yard when the immigrants turned up, cruising through the Brewsters' stomping grounds in a battered van. The family watched the van hit the dead end, down where the keep out signs begin, and it stopped. The doors opened. Everybody piled out.

"Why, there's that interesting family again. Isn't that the interesting little family we saw in town?"

"But why do you suppose so many strangers show up here," Jason asked, "when they're just a few miles from a public beach?"

"We mustn't judge. I know I try not to. We must be tolerant. It takes all sorts."

The woman kept the children from milling very far. The parents stared at the signs, obviously discussing the matter.

Lyle appeared. "Why don't you tell them they can walk on the beach, Ma! Jesus Christ! How could that hurt?"

"We can't always do just what we would like. Those stairs are old, in bad shape, and who's going to be responsible when someone falls? I know I can't be, with my bills."

The mother finally herded everybody back to the van. "Come on," she kept saying, in generally unaccented English. "We've got the picture cards! We've got the picture cards!"

The Brewsters held their breaths, but the father was evidently used to sandy stretches. He turned successfully, avoiding the shoulders. Then they were gone.

"Well," Jason said, "that's that. Could anybody here use a drink? I know I could. Besides Charley, of course."

5 / Nerves

*J*ason brought his fiancée to meet the family the following summer, and Charley saw her first. He was alone in the house when Jason called from the airport, and he picked them up at Race Point. Suzanne Fletcher dressed stylishly even on the scruffy Cape: flowered cotton skirts and flouncy, open-necked blouses. She did not appear to own any jeans. She was in her middle thirties, with blondish hair cut short, fluffed up to frame a narrow, tense-looking face. She had her son with her, a close-cropped, sharp-boned six-year-old from a recently broken marriage. (Her ex-husband, an accountant, had turned gay and was living with a rug merchant in a Chicago high-rise.) She was appreciative and enthusiastic. She admired everything she was shown and fell in love with Truro. "Oh, just *imagine* living here! Just the view! Wouldn't anyone scrub *floors* just to stay! Wouldn't I help clean the cottages?" However, there was something constructed and brittle about these enthusiasms, as if she had been alerted, or coached, and the strain showed. She was soon being sincere, and defiantly so, as if she did not care and could not help herself.

She was opinionated and fastidious. She couldn't bear the sand fleas, for instance. The family arranged the cocktail hour around the sunsets. They carried their drinks out to the patio as soon as the light softened, but while this was transpiring, she stayed inside with Jason, peering out. The family could see them in the windows.

The situation was strained, if not at first commented upon, and the family did not vary its routine at that hour. They rated the sunsets as usual, giving them from one to ten, and they clapped when the sun finally disappeared. They gradually drifted back to the house for fresh drinks, blinking and stumbling about as if they had just come from an absorbing play; but at the same time they now felt curiously self-conscious and resentful, children sensing a tacit form of disapproval. As a result, the drinking picked up. (Charley was drinking again, but trying to keep it at a reasonable level.)

She did not eat seafood, which certainly limited the menu; when the boys came, they ate little else. "I just think of it as so undeveloped," she said. "You know, not finished. It is, though, isn't it, an acquired taste?"

Her son was always ready to get an argument going. "Fish is brain food," Eric said.

"Mother doesn't know, dear. Mother doesn't touch it."

"Yes, it is. I know. I read that." He looked around the table, wanting admiration. "Isn't that right?"

"Eric? Sweetheart? Please? *Do* you think you could eat a little more slowly? Would you like to think about it? Do you remember our talk about the digestive system?"

If she hovered over him a great deal, as if he were the incomplete product of a fragile relationship, Eric appeared to be both self-sufficient and foolhardy. "I'm going to learn to swim soon," he announced, when he first saw the bay. Then he walked in, past the chin, as if he were about to get started. Jason had to pull him out.

Wary of children, Charley kept his distance. In fact, he could not get himself to touch one. He was seeing a counselor, and the shrink had asked him to locate an early snapshot in an effort to reach his childhood. Charley brought it in his wallet, taken in Truro when he was about Eric's age, a chubby, somber-looking being whose smile seemed forced, older than his years. That same adult stance, the effort to please or placate, turned up in the set shoulders. He was standing beside an overturned dory, lobster traps and fishing gear in the blurred background, but in the formal attire (shirt, tie, knickers), he did not appear to be connected to the scene, and he couldn't remember the dory.

Charley and Dr. Struckmeyer pored over the picture together in downtown Lynchburg, Iowa, where the street in front of the office building was being ripped up; and while the men out there were busy with jackhammers, Charley was supposed to address the boy directly. He had not yet managed to say much, but given the queerish feelings such efforts elicited, he assumed he was getting somewhere. When Struckmeyer's clients were well, or at least functioning better, the doctor kept their childhood pictures. The ghostly, exorcised figures hung in neat rows behind his desk, like trophies.

Charley was actually ambivalent about Eric. The boy was bright, like him. He was filled with information. He would learn something about the Cape from Jason, and five minutes later he was lecturing someone less fortunate. He was a smart ass, too, like Charley. He could be amusing, from a safe distance.

Charley was going down to the water when Eric, Jason and Suzanne were coming up. She was trying to get the boy to put his shirt back on, and when he wouldn't, she dropped that topic for another. "But, darling," she was saying, trying to reach his hand without success, "do you think it's wise to carry sharp shells around in your pockets? What if you fell? Would you like to think about that?"

The boy looked mystified, an obvious act. "Shells? What shells? They're slipper limpets, to be precise, and, yes, I believe it's wise. I have too many to carry."

"But, darling, whatever. Isn't the point the same?"

"These are true mollusks," he insisted, still holding forth when Charley was out of range.

Myra was planning on some free entertainment. The Donaldsons had brought up a houseguest that year, an African. He was a Harvard musicologist and an amateur flutist.

Julia allowed as how she was not unimpressed, either. "He's better looking than Harry Belafonte. Why is he limiting himself to Harvard?"

"I'm not into looks," Myra said, as if she had not noticed.

Charley was interested in the outcome. The man's voice was too precisely soft to suit him, the detached, faraway manner too amused. Wouldn't he turn her down flat?

He did not. Perhaps obligated to the Donaldsons, or perhaps curious about the patio rites, he showed up with his flute. That night the sunset was particularly lurid, given nine points. The musicologist offered a little Vivaldi, bringing the sun down safely, at no cost, and then he excused himself. The Donaldsons followed. When the remains of color scattered, the darkness seemed beneficent, a kind nothingness. Myra broke the spell. "Well," she said, looking around for the musicologist, "we have all had a rare treat. I know I have."

Darwin appeared with fresh drinks, and Misty stood.

Misty had said nothing when Charley had started drinking again—a bad sign. She was drinking more herself these days. He did not know precisely why he thought so, but ever since the miscarriage, he sensed that more went on inside than met the eye, or ear. He sensed a certain self-destructive willfulness. She was a thwarted romantic. But this condition seldom changed the romantics' view of the world; they merely went around the offending object, chin up, eyes lifted toward the horizon.

Jason had taken his intended into town that night, and without the usual pressures the family got fairly noisy. They clumped back and forth from the patio to the house, carrying sweaters, bug repellents, fresh drinks. Lyle stoked the open fire. When Myra finally left, he fell into the flow. He had a drink and found some old fireworks. The first set fizzled, the next was satisfactory, and everyone clapped. Jerry produced a transistor, and some people danced. Figures circled in the dimness, partly visible when close to the fire.

Misty got a little drunk, and her eyes filled with tears. She was dancing by herself. She was wearing a sweater, but, if chilly, she was still in the day's running shorts. The long, thin, calfless legs showed deep brown when she passed the fire. Charley told her she was beautiful, and instead of protesting, she nodded, as if that were one more mysterious fact in a world of many. She stopped suddenly, spreading out her arms. "This is my family," she said. "All of you. You're *all* here!"

Everybody applauded and Jerry hugged her. They danced, briefly. Jerry had a roving eye, but Misty had no specific interest in men. "All right, you two," Charley said, "easy on the intimacy here." The remark was detached, obligatory. People clapped again.

Wide-eyed, trying to get through, Misty was still standing by the open fire. Sparks flew up behind her. "No, now, I'm *serious!* I don't care! I'm having fun," she said, but was actually growing melancholy. "What we've got to do in the future, though, is try to include Suzanne. Would that hurt? Is she such a *bad* person?"

People clapped. They agreed she was, absolutely. They drank to Misty, they drank to Suzanne. She kept trying to get through, close to heavy weeping now. "Honestly! You *people!* Have you tried *hard* enough with her? Can you really say you have?" She finally changed everybody's mind. People shuffled around in their chairs, ready to quit. Charley put his hand on her shoulder. She looked at him for a moment as if she did not know who he was. Then she said "Time to leave?" He nodded. When they left, the rest followed.

Charley broke his glasses in the shower the next morning.

"In the *shower?*" Julia said, at breakfast.

Misty did not appear to be hung over *or* apologetic. "Those kinds of things happen to him. I don't ask."

He limped around in a discarded pair of glasses he had found, his before he had hit his twenties. The outdated prescription caused considerable eye strain, and when he looked out, the shifting, blurry spaces increased his sense of disorientation.

Julia and Misty had a project in mind. They decided that the adults were taking Suzanne into Wellfleet for lunch. Jerry started to argue. He didn't know why the women couldn't just go. Julia didn't give *that* suggestion the time of day. "You're going, and that's that. We're all going. We're all going to enjoy ourselves, too," she said, sounding like Myra.

Feeling safe, Charley set off to find his mother. He would

tell her about the day's plans first, giving the news time to sink in. Second, as an alternative, he would ask her to drive him down to the family optician in Hyannis instead. She enjoyed Hyannis, didn't she? She liked getting out.

He found her in the new cottage, getting ready for the L. L. Bean couple. Lyle had been working hard through the spring, and everything smelled of fresh paint. She was busy tacking up her famous notices: suggestions, admonishments and subtle threats which were meant to make life easier on everyone.

> Welcome to this little home.
> We hope you treat it as your own.
>
> If you smash or break a dish,
> We hope you replace it.
> That's our wish!!
>
> Please do not put Kleenex or
> Paper towels in the hopper.
> Only toilet tissue's proper.

According to Myra, the L. L. Bean couple was well heeled. They had taken the place for the season. According to Myra, all her guests had at least a little money, liked music and leaned appreciatively toward the other arts. In any case, even if the L. L. Bean woman was tone deaf, Charley could not imagine her stuffing Kotex down the stool on the sly; she was past fifty, anyway. But his mother, despite her optimism, was always cautious. "Better be safe than sorry"—that was her other side.

While he was explaining, she seemed to be listening. She looked at him straightforwardly enough. "I'll just finish up here first," she said. That was all. As if his was certainly a simple request.

But nothing was simple in that house. When she reached the kitchen, she had her head cocked to the side, her eyes half-closed, the expression dimmed out. She had her ruminative posture. "I've decided we'll make a day of it. We'll take the children along."

"The *children?* You're kidding. What on earth for?"

"I don't get a chance to be alone with them enough when they're here. This is an opportunity."

"And *all* of them?" he asked, intentionally making it sound like hundreds. "Aren't you going to have to stack them in like cordwood?"

She said that she couldn't leave anyone out, could she? Could he say that was fair, honestly? Once she got an idea into her head, there was no trying to remove it, either. Arguing with her was like arguing with a brick wall.

He resigned himself to the trip. Conscious of his limits, he knew that, once in his life, he ought to consider trying to confront his fears. And a fear of children was ridiculous. The phobia probably did not even have a name. He would watch himself closely throughout the day and then give a full report to Struckmeyer when he got back to Iowa. They would go over every detail carefully together.

Julia looked dubious. Also harried. She was calling around for noon reservations at the last minute. "Myra can't handle six children alone. She'll lose the last of her marbles before she's halfway there."

"Charley's going, too," Jerry said.

"*Those* two? Really? Are you *serious?* Together?"

Charley was miffed. "We're just going to Hyannis, Julia, *not* China."

"Well, all right, but you'll have to bash a few heads together, just to keep the day pleasant. I'll give them some last-minute instructions."

Myra was taking the station wagon. She put the back seat down to accommodate the six: Jerry and Julia's son (now five); Jerry's two girls from his second marriage (eleven and twelve); Jason's two sons from his first (eight and ten). Eric was watching the procedure. He scrambled on last. "Suzanne prefers seat belts," he observed, impressed with the change.

Myra was still searching for her keys. She did not look up. "Seat belts?" she asked, vaguely. "What do you suppose people did before seat belts, Eric? They sat quietly in their corners, didn't they? They didn't ask questions."

She couldn't find the car keys and went back to the house to look. That was par for the course. Charley fidgeted in the front seat. He should have known better than to try to settle himself in so soon. The children, though, were quiet. They sat back there in the simmering heat without fussing, probably still remembering Julia's last-minute threats, and under some shock.

Julia appeared with Myra. She brought the car keys down. "I know everybody's going to look after each other. I know I'm expecting good reports."

"Yes, yes. Where's Mother now?"

"She's looking for her shopping list."

"*Shopping?* She didn't say anything about shopping."

"She says she's making a day of it."

He groaned. "Just get her down."

"I've got to get Jerry organized next."

Jerry was a wonder, given his divorces, but he had a hopeful ethic. When a relationship sours, a man can move on. Like Myra, he did not dwell on the past. Myra, in fact, erased it. Searching for the picture of himself in her photograph albums, he discovered that she had carefully edited the truth over the years until she had eliminated life's less-flattering angles. Blurry areas, like rising ectoplasmic traces, showed up where his father's pictures had been removed. She had also cut the captain from group shots, the balloonlike spaces now hovering forms that emphasized absences.

Myra returned. She sat behind the wheel with the motor running, going through her shopping list.

"Mother? How about it? *Could* we get this show on the road?"

"Hold your horses," she said, backing up without looking behind. "We're going to have a nice, leisurely trip."

He had forgotten how Myra drove. She barreled up and down Truro's hills and hollows, moving onto 6A without pausing, and Highway 6, always frantic, did not phase her, either. She did not signal. Following eastern customs, she let anything in the rear take care of itself. After his years in Iowa, he had trouble adjusting to this less-advanced civilization. He thought about buckling up, but he could not get himself to do so, with the children rattling around in back. How would it look if only he survived the wreck?

Eric had stuffed his pockets with shells before leaving, and he pulled them out now, spreading them on the floor between his legs. Myra glanced in the rearview mirror. "You'll pick up those shells when you've finished, won't you, dear? We all want to be tidy."

"Watch the road, Mother, please."

She was in high spirits. "Let's see what we can see, children. Let's sit back! We'll all have stories to tell when we return, won't we?"

There was not much to see and would not be throughout the trip: just shrub, some patches of sand, gas stations, package stores, novelty shops and tourist cabins back in among the pines. These usually advertised some water, but you could not see it from the highway. His eyes teared behind the outdated prescription, and he turned from the window, trying to get comfortable sitting sideways.

Jerry's two girls, older than anybody else (older than God, they thought), had not wanted to come in the first place. They bored quickly. They claimed they did not have enough space and started fighting between themselves. Some mild pushing was involved. The argument was still low key, but could turn ugly.

Myra either ignored them or did not hear them. He realized that she was growing a little deaf lately, but he did not want to think about that. He knew he should say something to the girls, but he did not know what.

They would soon feel too adult to be a part of any family vacation, and they would cease coming to the Cape at all. They would be off on their own, in some corner somewhere, getting pregnant. But, of course, these summers themselves would eventually end. People would die, and in the process, Myra's hill would change, the eighteenth-century farmhouse torn down or remodeled. Garish motels would start to appear where her cabins had been.

The argument in back picked up steam. Myra glanced in the mirror. "What were the promises we all made? Who remembers the promises?"

The girls glanced at each other. They glowered, but stopped. "But we wanted to go slumming around today at Race Point," Jerry's younger said. "Julia said we were going, yesterday." The other nodded. They were a team when not fighting.

Jason's two took this in. "Slumming?" the elder asked. "What's slumming? I thought we were going swimming." Jason's boys were still too young to horse around with females yet. They would probably skip that stage, anyway, being Jason's. Both darkish and handsome now, they looked impressively repressed.

Myra was still looking in the rearview mirror. "Well, we've changed our plans. We're going shopping."

Charley frowned. "Just watch the road. I want to arrive whole."

She looked back at the road, briefly. "Nerves," she said. "That's your trouble. You have *such* nerves."

The wagon's air conditioning had kept him comfortable up in front, but the mall parking lot was a heated pit. He moved with his head down, his eyes watering, half-shut. The children followed reluctantly, spread out.

Myra turned. "Stay close, everybody. This is one family. Take hands."

He had planned separating at the optician's, but she wanted to keep the group together, and they all filed into the place, an adventure. She needed to catch her breath. She sat down in the reception area, her big purse on her lap, fanning herself, trying to strike up a conversation with the receptionist. "My, this is nice, isn't it? It's so cool in here. We're having an outing," she explained. "We're making a day of it. These are my grandchildren."

The gaunt, hollow-eyed woman behind the counter tried to look interested. "My, and don't you have a lot?" She patted the back of her head.

They milled around, picking up things, disorganizing the magazine rack. Jerry's older girl was standing on one foot, trying to scratch her ankle with the other. "Can we go swimming as soon as we get back?"

"Why are we scratching ourselves in public? Do little ladies do that in public?"

Eric gravitated toward the reading matter. He sat down with a Rotary Club magazine, elbows resting on the chair arms, feet swinging clear of the floor. "I'm a house guest. I'm from Chicago. My father's living with his friend."

Myra leaned over toward him, her hands still on her purse in her lap. "Well, we all need friends, don't we, dear?" She patted his knee, quickly, then put her hand back on her purse. "Don't bother the people here."

The optician finally turned up. Well past middle age, he was tanned to a dark, walnut-colored stain, and deeply lined. The massive, ball-shaped, kinky white hair that framed his face looked fake but was not. "Well," he said, to Myra, "what have all the years been doing to everybody?"

"Life starts at sixty-five. So they tell me."

Charley put his broken glasses down on the counter, and she started to explain what needed doing. "He wanted to keep those frames. You want to keep those frames, don't you. Charley? He broke them in the shower."

The optician ignored the glasses, as if business was not yet on his mind. He leaned forward on the counter. "Tell me, now, Myra, do these boys of yours ever see their father?"

She pursed her lips against the intrusion. "I have raised them all without help. I know that I have had to pray a lot."

"Well, you're a Christian, Myra, and *he* was always a wanderer. The captain liked to get around. Been all over the world, they tell me."

She set her mouth again. "*They* say a lot. I can't always keep up."

Jason's youngest stood in the middle of the room clutching his groin. Myra leaned forward, still holding her patent leather purse. "Could you use a facility? I think you could use a facility." She looked at the receptionist. "I think he could use a facility. Everybody go while we're here. Everybody take advantage. Use the facilities."

Despite their complaints about the heat, the children dragged their feet when they saw the next stop coming up. The discount house was freezing, and Charley groaned when he saw the lines. "Do we *have* to go here, Mother? It's *packed.*"

She could smell a sale a mile off, and under this spell, she was alone. "Everybody wants some action."

Jerry's son wanted to ride in the cart. The girls fought over who was going to push him. They wanted something to drink.

"We'll see," Myra said, not hearing. "Everybody look for plastic dish sets." She was still furnishing the L. L. Bean place. She wanted the cottage to look its best.

Eric stuck close to Jason's sons, and if there was a considerable age difference, they did not appear to notice. He was lecturing them on shells. He had difficulty getting the shells out of his pockets and keeping his shorts up at the same time. Jerry's son wanted to be in on this, and he leaned over the edge of the basket, trying to grab the shells. Just out of the boy's reach, Eric held out his arm and unclenched his fist. "Slipper limpets, and they're true mollusks."

"I wouldn't give them to him if I were you," Myra said, as if the boy were still an infant. "He might put them in his mouth."

Eric stopped to adjust his shorts, trying to get them pulled back over his hipless shape. Then he had trouble with a shoe. While he stood on one foot, he grabbed Charley's hand for support. Charley was pleasantly surprised to note that his own hand responded. What was he feeling? He was feeling helpful.

Jerry's younger girl glanced at Myra. "He isn't supposed to scratch himself in public, is he?"

"He *isn't,*" Charley said. "He's fixing his shoe."

Eric was not conscious of Charley's various feelings, of course, and as soon as he had his balance back, he dropped his hand. "Do we have many bugs up here? I think I'm going to study bugs next."

"Not my bugs," the girl said.

Myra turned. "Let's everybody keep up. We don't want to get separated."

The supermarket was even more crowded than the discount

house had been. There were long lines at the produce stands and at the check-out counters, and she was determined to cover a week's shopping. He tagged along without arguing. What was the use?

The girls headed toward the Coke dispensers, but Myra said she did not make a habit of pouring perfectly good money into those machines, as if she were discussing Las Vegas. "I know we all want to watch our pennies," she said.

They passed the seafood station. "I would like to try some fish," Eric said.

Jerry's son was growing tired of the cart. He squirmed, stretching out his hand toward the oysters. "Fish?" he said.

"Suzanne doesn't care for fish," Eric explained. "She says it's too elemental."

"Following that logic, she ought to prefer human flesh."

Eric stopped, intrigued. "Like cannibals?" He studied his arm, then lifted it up, chewing on the skin, tenderly. "Here's Suzanne," he said, looking around, waiting for some signs of appreciation.

Jason's son squealed. He tried his arm.

Myra was still in her dreamy state. "We all must remember where we are," she said, looking as if she did not. "We're all little ladies and gentlemen."

Eric was persistent. "But fish is good for you. Fish is brain food."

Myra only purchased hers directly from the docks. "Certainly nobody with brains would eat this."

Considering Suzanne, how could Eric be so bright? Charley was soon thinking about the differences between parents and children, people who could still share common bonds. He compared his father's high school education with his own Ph.D. in comparative literature. His father had just about finished high school at that, but according to all accounts, he was supposed to be bright. He had read some, once, judging from the books still in Myra's attic. "Mother," he asked, out of nowhere, "aside from *wandering,* what did he do? What was he like?" He could never get himself to say the word *father* aloud. Jason could, but Jason was an emotional idiot. Jason had long since managed to bury his feelings under elaborate sentiments. When any amount of truth threatened to come through, he could always whip a maxim forth.

The good thing about Myra was you never knew where her mind was at any given moment, and she never worried about where someone else's might be. At least nothing out of context ever surprised her. "I don't know. I can't say. He was never at home enough to know."

Charley wasn't ready to quit. "What did he think about having five boys?"

"Did he know? He could step over his children without seeing them. Certainly he never noticed you were always under my feet."

You also never knew when she was going to turn so forthright. She paused now, looking reflective, as if she had more to contribute along those lines. But he was no longer interested. He didn't want her to rattle on. "Let's get going, if we're going."

"I still need some dish soap. What about cereal?"

He removed his glasses and rubbed his eyes. He could sense a headache coming. He felt enclosed, cut off, but not nearly enough so. The children, the place, were beginning to get to him, and he wanted a drink. He *needed* a drink.

When they reached the check-out counter, the children headed for the candy rack. She finally bought a packet of assorted sours and passed them around while she was talking to the clerk. "I have all my grandchildren with me," she explained. "It's a big day. We're having an outing."

The clerk leaned forward. "Please pass those onions down to me, will you, honey?" she asked in a weary voice.

While they were stacking the groceries in the wagon, Myra told him she was thinking about going to McDonald's. He was not, but as usual, there was no point in trying to debate the issue. She always had her own logic worked out. ("If we get them fed now, we can ignore them later. I won't have to bother.")

At McDonald's there were a lot of bathroom trips before they could get settled, and because the place was filling up, Charley staked out a table while this procedure was in full swing. She instructed the older ones to help the younger ones, but they merely raced ahead. Then, once inside a stall, someone had trouble unlocking the door.

When they were assembled, if that was the word, they announced their orders in detail, talking at once, shouting above each other, several times changing their minds. Myra was letting them load up, saving her the fuss later. There was no gin on the menu, of course, and as if he had been expecting to find some there, Charley was furious with the place. He got up to stand in another line. While he waited, he removed his glasses and rubbed his eyes. By now his headache was serious.

When he returned, the girls were arguing again, snapping back and forth. Even Jason's two showed the strain. They were trying to shove each other out of the booth.

While he was passing the food around, his mother went into her standard litany. "Where are all the little ladies and gentlemen?" she kept asking, glancing here and there. "*I* don't see any little ladies and gentlemen. Where have they all gone?"

The food briefly slowed them down, and Eric grew reflective. He was staring out at the garish clown, the playground and the passing traffic. His pale green eyes suddenly sparkled with interest. "We *stole* all this from the Indians, didn't we?"

The boy was too much for Myra. She did not care for him, and as the day wore on, she had made fewer bones about it. "Why, *no!*" she said now, put out. "Where did you ever get such an idea?"

The girls devoured their food in minutes flat. They glanced around to see if anybody was going to leave any.

Eric was disapproving and a smart ass about it. "You're not supposed to gobble your food. You're supposed to eat very slowly, like this," he instructed, a parody of Suzanne. He exaggerated the pauses between each bite. When another table looked up, he further slowed the action down.

Charley's wallet was still out on the table, and Jerry's boy wanted it. Charley passed it over to keep him quiet. He soon had Charley's identification, credit cards and pictures all over the table.

Myra picked up the snapshot of the lost child standing beside the dory. "Why, that's Jason," she said.

Charley snatched the picture back. "No, that is *not* Jason."

"Well, of *course* it is! I clearly remember those knickers."

He realized that, even if she was wrong, she had certainly rendered the picture worthless.

The girls had gotten into Eric's shells. Bored, looking for some action, they pushed them across the table, pretending the shells were alive, creeping around, talking to each other. Then embracing.

Jerry's boy wanted part of the action. He threw the wallet down and leaned over the youth seat, trying to reach the shells. His face turned purple. "Mollsocks?" he kept saying. "Mollsocks?"

"They're true mollusks," Eric explained.

Then Jerry's boy tipped his orange drink. Half the room turned to stare, as if happy to witness this criminal act. Enraged, frightened, beside himself, the boy was still screaming when an attendant appeared with a mop.

Ignoring the chaos, intent on their own world, the girls were still pushing the shells back and forth.

Charley was close to the edge. "God *damn* it, anyway, *will* you put those *fucking* mollsocks *down!*"

They hastily retreated in several directions, split up, taking different doors.

Myra mentioned his choice of language once but fell quiet in the car, if humming was quiet. She hummed all the way home. The children alternately dozed and stared into space. He was numb. He was thinking about the drink he was shortly going to build for himself. When they reached the house, the children gradually came to. They sat up slowly, looking around them. They claimed they could not find Eric.

Myra was stuffing keys and Kleenex in her purse. "Well, I'm sure we're all here," she said, sounding out of it.

Charley checked, then froze. "*Mother! Mother! Mother! Wake up,* will you? We've got to go back!"

She suddenly looked feeble and old, as if she had lost the last of her bearings. "I'm still your mother. I'm your mother, and you've never raised your voice to me before. My children have never done that."

Her strongest emotion was self-pity, and under that power she was safely sealed off. He suddenly saw, in her, his own impaired lot, his squints, tics and secrets.

His brothers appeared on the porch. Coming down, the others following—a delegation—Jerry opened his mother's door. "McDonald's called. The women went down to get him." He was whispering. She continued to sit behind the wheel while Charley and the children climbed out. "Suzanne, of course, was unreasonable. Mother?" he continued to whisper, as if after a lot of shouting.

"I can't see any point in going over what Suzanne said," Jason said. They were all whispering.

Jerry was still standing by his mother's door. "I was proud of Jason. Mother? Let's go in."

"All my life," she said, looking dazed, as if ready to be told what to do, "all my life." She stayed where she was.

"Wouldn't have worked out anyway, Charley," said Jason. "Better face the problem now than later."

"Charley?" asked Jerry. "You all right? Charley's quiet."

The horizon by now held a pale salmon wash, but the air was still warm. He had to take sympathy from Jason, but he decided that was his due. He went around to his mother's side. "Come on, then, Mother." She remained where she was.

Lyle came down last, speaking in his normal voice. "What's going on?" he asked, shouting. "What's going on? What's holding everybody up?"

The others turned. "Help here," Jerry said. "Mother's not moving."

Lyle broke through. She pulled herself together. "Stop *shouting*," she said. "Stop shouting. I can *hear* you!"

Lyle ignored her. "Everything's going to be fine now," he kept saying. "Yes, yes, yes! We're all here! We're all together! We're all back! We're all home!"

6 / The Garden of Love

*M*yra had taken the day off before the summer started and the family arrived. She did not even have Lyle on her hands. Jason had driven him to Disney World with his two boys, and he was bringing him back when he came up. She was more reclusive than people realized, certainly more reclusive than her family realized, and she was owed this time to herself. All her life she had done for others, starting with her mother's death, leaving her to run the house, her father's servant. Then there was the captain, and the five boys started coming. She had married a Catholic who, in fact, did not particularly want children, or did not notice their presence; but he never thought about the next day or any consequences in general—that type—and his religion was his excuse. Her father and that man had been alike in many ways, two peas in a pod. There was nothing in them that was there to handle children; where a man should have been, there was just another child needing attention. When they didn't get their way, there was a scene, or worse.

They both had their little airs, too. Her father worked in a factory, but he had Old World notions, and he did not associate with the other men. The "captain" called himself that, but wasn't. He had actually been a fishing guide at his best, squiring rich Republicans around the South Seas during the depression. Aside from that, he chased cod around Georges Bank like anybody else. He claimed that he had been all over the world many times, but if he had seen the South Seas, he had not seen much else. He had never seen Europe. In fact, he had never bothered to see Boston.

Unlike her father, he certainly drank. When he was drinking, he talked to himself, or sang off-key. Coming in the front door, into the small, cramped hall, climbing the steep, narrow steps, he swayed from side to side as if still steadying himself against churning seas. "I'm *back!*" he roared, once home (as if anyone cared), back to the family hearth from all parts of the world. Or so he claimed. "I'm here! I've returned!" Then halfway up the stairs, he paused to catch his breath. "Oh, I found a lemon in the garden of love, where they say only roses grow," he sang, always off-key, his favorite piece. Feeling around in his pocket for matches, trying to get his cigar lit.

In deference to some tradition, he did not drink in the house. He kept a bottle in the tackle shed in back, and when he was feeling his oats, he could spend the better part of the day going back and forth between the shed and the kitchen, where he fussed over his fish stews. He seasoned strongly, stirring in the tails and the heads. Unshaven, his baseball cap on backwards, chewing a dead cigar. "Oh, I found a lemon in the garden of love," he sang, "where they say only roses grow."

He did not belong in this day and age. He did not drive a car. He had refused to learn, as if driving were beneath him, and when he went to church, Myra had to bring the car around. He went once a year, on Easter, but that meant two trips. She had to take him to confession first. He needed fortification before he could get himself out of the house, and he first visited the tackle shed. He never spoke in a normal tone of voice, but, when fortified, he shouted as if he were at a helm barking out orders over high winds; and when he was in a confessional, people could hear him all over the church. The priest could not get him to lower his voice. But those priests weren't like good Protestants, and when they noticed the drinking, they merely appeared to be amused. They did not consider it to be a sin.

He was generally talkative, filled with more information than anybody wanted to hear, and since he was pleased with himself after confession, by then wound up, he tried to keep the priest cornered. He was interested in the world's great mysteries: the gulf currents and the ocean beds, dying suns and distant planets, magnetic forces and migrating birds, carnivorous plants and killer ants, ghost ships and saints' relics, roving vampires and all grieving, restless spirits.

She could never understand Catholics. They did not seem to want to get ahead. He seldom shaved, and changed his shirt less. Without her, he would not have saved a cent. Self-absorbed and dreamy, concerned with the higher things, she had kept her eyes on real estate. (That accounted for the cottages.) She enjoyed the shop talk, what people were getting for an empty lot these days, or what any shed would bring with a water view. ("Nice two-bedroom starter home," for instance. "Needs some fixing up: $195,000.")

She couldn't see the sense in that scrubby, open expanse, herself, and when she considered retirement, her mind had more recently turned to Brewster or Dennis, where the towering trees and town squares reminded her of what New England *should* look like. She liked things nice, and as far as she was concerned, the Truro moors and clay cliffs were just depressing. The wind blew steadily through the winter months, tearing everybody's shingles loose, and until the tourists appeared in summer, unless you counted Bingo, there was no social life.

She was rambling around now, checking on real estate before she had lunch and caught up with her shopping. She got the agent out to look at a place in Dennis—a small, white-haired woman in a stretchy blue polyester pants suit, showing the fat. Mrs. Hodges also owned a gift shop, which was closed at that time of year, but she had her office overhead. Myra had to wait until the woman found the right key. She seemed scatterbrained, but Myra decided this could be part of an act. She stayed on her guard around all real estate people. They were not against asking for anybody's eyeteeth.

On the way over, Myra let her know that she was not an outsider, some foreigner from Connecticut or New Jersey. She said she had a considerable investment in Truro now, and because of what *that* could bring, she knew about the inflated prices. The woman did not treat her like a customer after that.

She treated her like a kindred spirit. She shook her head in commiseration. "Old people around here," she said, "old people with land for years? They can't keep it in the family anymore. They're forced to sell, like it or not, because they can't afford the taxes."

Myra sat up straight beside her in the front seat, her hands across her patent leather bag, her mouth pursed. "I'm not exactly in that shape," she said.

The woman talked a blue streak. "A tourist walked up to this house last summer he liked? This stranger's house, with no sign in the yard? And rang the bell. Says, 'What do you want for this place?' Well, '*What?*' the woman says, not following, and he has to repeat himself. 'What do you want for this house?' She was insulted. She told him it wasn't up for sale. Just, you know, wasn't, but after four or five visits, she named a price. He took it, too, without question."

While the agent continued to talk, Myra rejected the half-Cape at a glance. The roof, gutters and drains needed repair. She found frayed carpets and water stains inside. The cramped rooms depressed her, considering her space at home, and she would not even dicker over the price.

Back at the gift shop, she climbed into her own car with a sharp sense of relief. She wasn't ready to make such a change yet. She had also managed to put off a major problem: Lyle. When she finally retired, she wanted to live alone, and nobody had ever bothered to explain to her just what she was supposed to do with him. When she talked about her other sons, she called them "the professionals," always adding that Lyle was still at home, as if he were still deciding on a profession. In fact, he had not finished high school. She wasn't going to dwell on that now, though. This was her day, and she was going to make the most of it.

She had lunch in a place on a backcountry road where from the bay window she could see a garden filled with late spring flowers, an inn with antiques, an open hearth and exposed beams. It was not seasonal. Many restaurants up Cape were not, because the area was filled with year-round couples, retired people with good pensions or living on stocks and bonds. They did not just appear in the summers, flooding the beaches and the gift shops. She was back for a moment imagining herself in some small half-Cape on a town square across from a Congregational church. She could imagine herself helping with rummage sales. She looked around for a waiter. She had heard the food was supposed to be exceptional, but because it was, the service was slow, the customers neglected in favor of some high ideal.

Wearing a backless purple dress, a young, heavyish woman came in alone with a child—a divorced woman, she supposed, and out of her element. The makeup was too lavish, but she probably never left the house without it, in case some opportunity should arise. The child immediately objected to the youth chair, and he was clearly going to be difficult. He certainly couldn't reach the table without it. She did not know why the woman couldn't be firmer.

When the yelling started, Myra decided she would help. "My," she said, leaning over toward their table, "where are all the little gentlemen today?" She looked around her, as if searching. "I don't see any little gentlemen here, do you?" She smiled at the woman. "This isn't a family place, is it?"

She ignored the look she got back because she had too much else on her mind. She took her shopping list out of her purse. She was going to do some pricing in the Hyannis discount stores. The Maplewoods, favorite tenants, family friends, were bringing a houseguest this year, a British scientist, and she decided she was going to spruce up their cottage with several fresh throw rugs.

When she finally reached home, Father Bandom was waiting for her on the front porch, and as soon as she saw him, she knew that something unpleasant was up, if not what. He smelled like tobacco smoke and cheap shaving lotion, as usual, and if he was supposed to be a man of God, she could not have said why. He did not disabuse her about the unpleasantness, either.

"We have some news here for you, Mrs. B. Just a little surprise. You have a visitor. Who's been away for some time." He held the screen door open for her, as if he were offering her *his* house. "Come in! Come in! Please! We have coffee on."

She pushed past, wondering how he could ever bring anything *but* unpleasant news. In any case, she had her own minister, and if she ever needed help, an unlikely event, she would certainly spare this man the bother.

He followed, as if he had to show her what there was to see. "Here we are! Here we are! Back in the kitchen, Mrs. B. He's come all the way from Maryland, a long bus trip." He put his hands up, palms out. "I'll leave you two alone. A lot to catch up on, between you. A lot to explain. You'll want to talk."

The captain was sitting at the kitchen table, chewing on a dead cigar, a coffee mug in front of him. The small, squinty eyes still looked mean, and as usual, he was unshaven. He had always been short and stumpy, made of gristle—what on others could be called muscle—but this had somewhat softened. He had also shrunken a bit.

The blood seemed to leave all her vital centers. Dead weight, she dropped into a chair. She had never let him know he riled her. She had just maintained her airy, peaceable way, avoiding trouble, as if his outlandishness did not register or have any effect whatsoever. In fact, she could not stand up to him. Like her father (the tyrant who had thrown fits, broken furniture), he made her feel heavy, sluggish, passive. She was shaking slightly. "I have made my peace with my life, as it is, now," she said, half to herself. "I have made my way. I have met my obligations. I have raised those boys. Nobody could say otherwise."

He slithered his chair back from the table, as if he were about to rise, but did not. "Been all over the world, Myra, been to the four corners, have seen all the wonders that there are to see. Nothing left. Have returned to hearth and home. Have come back to die," he said.

The captain made a point of telling her he did not need much. Once he found his old baseball cap, he did not even bother the few possessions he had left around the house. As if it were a point of honor, he did not touch her food. He kept a fish stew simmering on the back of the stove, the flame turned low, and when he ate, which was seldom, he dished himself a bowl. Then he ate standing, as if her kitchen any other way imprisoned him. He disappeared as soon as he was through, leaving the bowl and the spoon in the sink. He appeared to have some resources of his own, because a bottle turned up in the tackle shed. When drinking, he still talked to himself, but the singing had stopped. He kept out of her way in general.

She certainly kept out of his as much as possible, which was not difficult to do. She was spending all her time on the cottages, getting them ready for the summer people. The cottages bothered him. The new patio angered him, too—the covered patio and the cement walks.

He stared at the patio, scratching his head, standing in a T-shirt that was torn at the back. "You got this place all fixed up, ain't you?" he said, amused. "A real little business on your hands. Just getting what you can from the summer people." He stood there, shaking his head. "She's a millionaire now," he said, still shaking his head. "Everybody in those places got their own bathroom, too. Toilets flush, every last one."

He had poked around more than she realized, but she should have known. She did not answer. She did not tell him that this was not *his* business anyway.

"What do you make on these places, Myra?"

"You wouldn't know anything about the mortgage I carry."

He chuckled. "What you need up here," he said, "is a good storm. Tear down the extras. Get back to basics."

She pursed her mouth without answering.

"You ever have any good *storms* up here anymore, Myra?"

"I've got work to do," she said. "I've got to get those cottages ready, and the family will be here soon."

He scratched his head. He took his cigar out of his mouth and studied it. "Where do they all sleep, the boys?" he asked. "You got room for the family, too? Where do you put them, in the cellar?"

She realized he had not mentioned his boys before.

The captain decided to move into the tackle shed. He claimed that he did not want to bother anybody, but he liked to think of himself as exiled out there—home, but still separate. He brought down a cot from the house. He cleaned out the shed, leaving what was not useful in the backyard. Myra worried about fire.

He generally did not pay much attention to what was said around him, as if he could not possibly be interested in that much ignorance; but if he decided to listen to somebody, he could pin him down with those squinty little eyes that still pierced, glowing pale green cold light. "Well, if there's a fire, then I'll burn," he said. "I may as well go one way as another. But when you see the fire starting toward the house, you can make up your own mind about that. You got a mind, ain't you? I can't take care of everything, Myra. I can't advise you day and night."

When she talked to the children about the summer plans, she did not mention the captain. She just acted natural. The captain was too much to go into over a phone, and besides she did not like to mention the unpleasant until she absolutely had to. She could cross that bridge when she reached it. In the meantime, ignorance was bliss.

Jerry and Julia arrived first. When they pulled off the road, the captain wasn't around, and she decided she wasn't going to raise the subject just yet. When he didn't show up at noon, she decided they were going to have a pleasant lunch, and she put off telling them.

While she was fixing a salad, Jerry wandered around the kitchen peering out. He always came up looking for changes. He wanted things to stay as they were, and he could spot any change. "What's been happening to the tackle shed, Mother? Why is all that junk in the yard?"

She was standing at the refrigerator door, her back to him. "Just some cleaning. I'm always cleaning" she said, sounding irritated.

"And you've been hauling those *tool* chests around? I bet you miss Lyle."

She said nothing. Considering the circumstances, she counted her blessings. She was glad he was not there. But *glad* wasn't a strong enough word. She had no idea how he would take it. He could have one of his little spells. As if she didn't have enough on her hands.

The captain didn't turn up that afternoon, either, but she was apparently beginning to show some strain because Jerry wanted to know what was wrong, and Julia agreed. "Well, *something's* going on," Julia said.

She intended to show a better front, and if they could get through the evening meal, she would tell them after the children were down, out of the way.

However, he came around the back of the house while she was fixing supper. The windows were open, and she could hear him whistling in the yard.

Jerry saw him first. Jerry was staring out the window, wearing a puzzled expression, and she realized the cat was out of the bag. "Who's that, Mother?"

She could hear the TV in the parlor. The children did not notice anything else when the TV was going, but just to make sure, she shut the doors—the one between the parlor and the living room, then the kitchen door. "Just to be on the safe side," she said.

"*What* safe side? What's going on?"

"That's your father. He's back. Everybody just act normal."

Jerry and Julia began to talk at once. She could not field all the questions, and she wasn't sure she cared to. "He's here," she said, "and that's that. He's here to stay."

"But *why*, Mother? Where did he come from? What's he said? What explanations has he given?"

She was only interested in the heart of the matter. "We're all going to make the best of it. We're going to be pleasant. We aren't going to argue. I know I am not."

"But do you mean *here*, permanently?" Julia asked. "*Surely* you're against that?"

She came close to breaking. She sat down at the kitchen table and wiped her face with her apron.

Jerry was insistent. "Well, Mother? *Aren't* you against it?"

"What can I tell him? What can I do? He's upset everything. *Nothing's* the same."

"Then *tell* him that! Tell him he *can't* stay!"

"What about the others, Mother? Who else knows? Who else has been told?"

She shook her head. "Your brothers don't know, and I don't want them to know, just yet."

"How's Lyle going to take it?"

"Well, we'll just have to cross those bridges when we come to them, won't we?" She felt calm again, and as far as the world was concerned, she was staying calm. "I want everybody to take this in stride. We're going to have a *pleasant* meal tonight. What shall we have that's really nice?"

Jerry wondered how he was going to respond when he first met the man. The captain had not come into the house that first night. He had not shown up at the evening meal—strain, of a sort—but since nobody was forcing the issue, Jerry was able to avoid meeting him there. As far as *he* was concerned, he did not care if he *ever* ran into him. That was his mother's problem.

When they were finally alone, Jerry worried about what Julia was going to say. He did not want to think about the whole situation himself, just yet. He did not want everything analyzed. He was dead from the road, anyway, and he just wanted to pass out. He crawled into bed hoping she would do the same.

In any case, she had not been speaking to him lately, and perhaps, just perhaps, she would not do so now. They had not been getting on these days. He had run into his brother's wife in the city, an innocent enough incident, but because Misty had wanted to talk, he had not caught the first plane back. His mistake was he had not instantly told Julia, and when he finally did, she was suspicious. She said that she did not exactly believe the worst, of course, but on the other hand, she still believed he wasn't exactly telling the truth, either.

She pulled her cotton flannel gown over her head now, but instead of getting into bed, she sat down on it beside him. "Well, what do you think?"

He was lying on his back. He switched to his side and pulled the blankets up to his chin. The light was still on, and he shaded his eyes with his arm. He knew the remark was just an opener. She was going to be telling him what *she* thought, and at length. "Can't it wait, Julia? I *have* no thoughts on the subject yet."

"All right. Let's just suppose she has herself in hand, which she has not, as much as she cares to *think* so. But let's suppose that. Do you see what she's *not* doing? She isn't considering you. She isn't considering her five sons. What about *their* feelings? Why does everybody just have to straighten up, for her?"

She paused. The light was bothering him, and he switched sides, his back to her. She leaned forward, and he realized she was reaching for the cigarettes on the bed table. She lit one, and he could smell the smoke. He was evidently in for a lot more. "But then *you* aren't trying to face your feelings yourself, are you?"

He was listening to the shades flapping back and forth at the open windows, blown by the strong cross breezes. "What am I feeling? I feel numb, Julia, just numb."

She put the cigarette out and angrily tossed back the covers until he was exposed to the chill. She meant him to be, too. For once, she was so angry, she couldn't even carry on about it. "All right, *sleep,* then! I give up!"

Chilly, brackish weather rolled in from the bay. The damp permeated the house, lingering in the sheets and the bath towels, and the plastic shower curtains turned sour. The children came down to breakfast in sweaters. Myra had toast under the broiler, and they rubbed their hands together in front of the open oven door.

No one mentioned the captain. Up and wandering around before anybody else, he had started the coffee, the only sign of his presence.

Myra was already planning lunch. Jerry was cleaning shrimp at the sink, keeping busy. By then it had started to drizzle hard, and every sea odor was emphasized. The shrimp smell lingered on his fingers, on his palms, and on the backs of his hands. "After this I was thinking of going to town. Does anybody need anything?"

Julia was getting the children's cereal down. "Trust you to cut out when I need the help."

He dropped the knife on top of the shrimp, lowered his head and leaned his elbows against the sink. "I wasn't *trying* 'to cut out,' as you put it."

"Well, then, what would you call it? I've got a lot of children cooped up."

Myra suddenly reached around and opened the window over his head. Jerry saw the man standing in the drizzle in front of the tackle shed, a dead cigar in the corner of his mouth, his hands in his back pockets. A coffee mug was sitting on a straight-backed chair just inside the tackle shed door.

"Dad! Dad! We're in here, at the window! There's someone to meet. This is Jerry."

The captain kept his hands in his back pockets. He nodded, stiffly, very formally, from where he stood, without moving any other part of his body. Other than this recognition, there was nothing. He did not speak.

Jerry was running tap water over the shrimp. His face set, expressionless, he nodded back. He felt pinned, frozen in the window frame.

Myra wasn't satisfied. "Aren't you going to come in, out of that wet?"

The captain was studying his son's face. He looked as if what he was thinking about him he was too polite to mention. "This isn't weather," he said. "This moisture? This isn't even *wet.*" He shook his head. He was chuckling to himself. He bent down to pick up the coffee mug behind him. "They don't know nothing about weather," he continued, as if addressing invisible friends, "and wouldn't, not in a million years." Then he walked off, into it.

The whiteness of the room (walls, ceiling, with its pitched roof), the open windows with their cross breezes blowing Myra's frail lace curtains. The sun was still strong. Naked, his stomach warm after his beach walk, so much exposure, his skin humming, burning (this side of burned because toughened), Jerry felt cold on the bed. He pulled up a sheet, tenderly, over his stomach. Because the room had so many windows (windows she had knocked through for the view, the breezes), so little wall space, the huge maple bureau sat catty-cornered between two walls. He could see himself in the bed in the bureau's oval mirror, framing his unshaven face above the sheet, the eyeglasses with big, dark frames.

The whiteness, the purity of the room, he thought, trying to describe it in his head. The light outside shining through the curtains, or falling directly in as the curtains flail out. The house was quiet. He could hear children's voices outside somewhere, and the tide in the distance, but muffled, like the distant sounds of traffic. He rolled over, reaching for his journal on the floor. Then settled himself back in the middle of the bed, propping the book up on his knees.

"The grays, the greens," he wrote, "all combinations, various hues, grays, greens, silver.

From up here, across the way, through the open window, in the empty field across from us, I can spot Queen Anne's lace, milkweed pods, a few cornflowers, a single clump of small daisies, the little color startling against the grays, browns, muted greens, the patches of sand. Then, beyond the cliffs, the frail, flat strip of blue, ruler-straight.

All day long the traffic passes on its way to the beach, that strip, the cars not doing ten miles an hour because of the ruts, potholes, in part, and because the drivers want to see everything. Then the walkers, around here usually old ones, slightly bent, hardly moving, carrying beach chairs, cotton blankets. Especially the old! Dear God! What do they *do* when they get down to the beach, except *look?* They'll even head down in inclement weather, on chilly, gray days, in the smudgy air, in sweaters, windbreakers. Going slowly, heads down, shaking some, watching their feet. Old, withered necks. Like a trip to Lourdes.

Given the general treelessness up here, the light on this end of the Cape is not diffused—hence its curious power. The sun, at five, is as concentrated as it is at high noon, but at five the sun falls horizontally. Just before I came up, standing at the screen door, I could feel the heat cutting me off at the knees, a burning sensation against the breezes. The wind whipping back grasses, silver where the light hits. The wind, now, smells like a freshly opened oyster.

The Cape is a series of austere, horizontal lines, and then the direct, undraped light. Kites everywhere. Caught in the phone wires overhead, standing out against the cloudless, azure sky above.

The back door opened, banged shut. The captain was in the kitchen, holding forth. Jerry put down his pen and closed his eyes.

Myra knew that the captain was running around a good deal with that priest. The man would show up at all hours, and then the two went to town. She had expected the captain to disapprove of Provincetown these days, considering the gay scene, but when he first came back, he sat in a corner of the kitchen chuckling to himself and shaking his head.

He had seen things he had never seen before, but he did not admit that, either. "Been all over the world, been to the four corners, have seen the great wonders, and so there's nothing new I need to learn, Myra. I *couldn't* learn nothing new," he said.

Despite the hours he kept, he was up at dawn. He banged the kitchen door, and while he was running the coffee water, rattling the plumbing, he woke the children. He could not be bothered with his grandchildren, and as soon as they appeared, he headed for the stairs. "Myra, there's a lot of *people* down here! Ain't you awake? You got your kitchen filled with *people!* They're running all over the place!"

She watched him from the kitchen window. He hung around the tackle shed through the late morning hours. The family passed from time to time, heading down the trail toward the bay in bathing suits. He stood watching with his hands in his back pockets, chewing his dead cigar. He studied this parade without speaking, as if even idiots could become subjects of some interest. He did not understand the beach life, and when he turned away, the expression said he did not care to, either.

He briefly turned up in the kitchen around noon when everybody was out. He dished himself a bowl of fish stew and stood in the middle of Myra's kitchen floor spooning it while in deep thought.

"Too bad you can just charge for those cottages, Myra. Too bad you can't charge for that water, too. You can put up a big fence, then take tickets. Every time anybody looks." He put his spoon and bowl down in the sink just before he stalked out.

He napped after lunch. He would stay out there in the shed until four or five o'clock, the family's brief respite. However, he kept the shed door open in case anybody was moving about, and if company showed up, he was soon back in the house.

She could count on his presence then. He wasn't going to miss a trick. She was talking to Dorothy Donaldson and her houseguest, the African flutist, when she heard the kitchen door. Her heart sank.

When he entered a room, he never stopped to address the occupants; he was always in the middle of some thought. "Why aren't you out there, getting the sun with the rest of them, Myra?" he asked, trying to stir up a little action. "Why ain't you in your bathing suit?"

The African looked amused. The captain studied him without seeming to. He was wearing a pastel-colored silk shirt and white pants, and the shirt, open at the neck, showed a gold chain. The captain had been briefly fascinated with the African. He had watched him from a safe distance, never addressing him directly but still marveling at the giant size. However, he gradually realized the African belonged to Myra, her built-in entertainment, and he wasn't currently interested. He did not believe that he was actually *from* Africa, anyway. He spoke with a Boston accent.

"Well? Why ain't you laying out there, too, Myra, half-naked?"

Dorothy Donaldson looked half-amused, never precisely sure how she was supposed to take him. She was a tall, tanned, keen-eyed woman who did not want to miss anything, but at the same time, she had a high, insecure-sounding laugh.

Myra ignored him as much as she could. "I have my cottages to run. You know that—at my age."

The captain stood there chuckling to himself and shaking his head. "You could get yourself one of them little *suits*, just straps. Show what you got. Everybody else out there, frying themselves up, showing what *they* got."

The flutist laughed outright. "That's the style, Captain."

The captain did not answer. He could not think of an answer at the moment. He went back to the tackle shed to check on his bottle.

Myra tried to start the conversation again. She could not remember what they had been discussing. She wanted to ask the flutist to play this year on the patio again, but she could not set a date until she knew the captain was going to be out of the house. Even when he went to town, he could show up at the last minute. He had a sixth sense.

The captain returned. He was louder. "Nobody," he said, "ever landed on any moon."

"Nobody here has mentioned the moon, Dad."

"Did you see it? Did you see it, with your own eyes? No, you did not. That was the television. It tells lies. It tells lies all the time. It's got things to sell, and it'll try to sell you anything, even the moon, providing you've got the money."

Dorothy tried to look interested, as if waiting to see what useful information was coming next, but her mouth was set.

"Now, Dad," Myra said, "you've been away a long time. You have a lot of catching up to do."

"Yes, and what *I've* seen doesn't come from any television. I can tell you that." He settled into his favorite topic. "Been all over the world, been to the four corners, have sailed the seven seas, and I have come back with the *facts*. Have seen native rites. Have studied the Easter Island heads, one of the world's great mysteries. Only thing anybody *here* knows is what he thinks he's seen on the TV."

The African's eyes sparkled. "*What* rites, precisely?"

Dorothy rose quickly. "Well, I know Myra has work to do."

The captain did not miss the man's sarcasm. He decided not to handle it directly. "You notice all the *nudists* around here, frying themselves up? Do you like the nudists?" His head was swimming some. He couldn't think of anything else to add at the moment, and when he had delivered his clincher, he left.

He appeared again when the coast was clear. He stayed on

the stoop this time, talking through the screen door. "Who did you say that colored fellow was?"

Myra was scouring the coffee pot. "I have told you, twice now. He's from Harvard. He's a visiting musicologist."

The captain chuckled. "I *told* you you didn't know no Africans, from Africa."

Jerry came up behind him. He was on his way upstairs to work on his journal. He had to squeeze past on the stoop, then wait until the man stood aside before he could reach the door. The captain took his time.

Myra was still trying to explain. "He studied music, Dad."

"Everybody around here went to college, including the Africans. They all went to college, but as far as I can tell, nobody here knows much. At least I haven't heard anything I would care to hear," he said.

Charley pulled in next.

Jerry was standing at the kitchen window when he saw the car. Myra was working in the utility room, and when he called her, she could not hear him at first over the washer.

Charley stepped out. The captain wasn't around. "Where's everybody? Is anybody *home?* We're off the road," he intoned, sounding like the captain, "and we need attention. Attention must be paid."

Julia turned when Myra appeared. "All right, they're here. Who's going to tell them? Who's handling this?"

"We'll have a pleasant lunch first. They'll have a lot to talk about."

"Myra!" Julia said. "*Now.*"

Myra dried her hands at the sink. "I'll keep it simple." She went out on the stoop, closing both doors behind her.

Jerry watched from the window, enjoying the various expressions. Myra's suggested a stern, artificial calm, as if she were in charge of keeping order during some great flood or storm.

Misty was wearing a rumpled white cotton skirt that accented her dark hair and skin. She looked puzzled, as if not taking the news in all at once. Or perhaps she was wondering how it could bear on her. Jerry had not seen his brother's wife since that curious evening in New York, when she had merely talked around some inner confusion or problem, and because of that intimacy, he saw her now as a stranger for the first time, having a life apart from his family's.

Charley was the wonder. He looked aloof and frozen, of course, masking obvious fury.

He came through the door first, still showing nothing. "How's everything, Jerry? Everything just about normal around here?"

Jerry was working on his journal upstairs.

Today I drove across the Provincetown line, then parked for a beach walk at low tide—past where the bay curves and the jumble of old houses begins. They are always changing shape, as if part of the flow, becoming from year to year increasingly difficult to identify. The fronts have been gouged out, usually on all floors, making room for every possible window (breezes, the view); they have been crisscrossed with raw wooden sun decks, porches, thin platforms (sunning, the view): the ravenous need to get in every inch. The sea was far out, the sun lulling, my striding effortless, and when I first realized where I was, I had already passed the church.

Summer weekend evenings are always the same in town. The movement is constant and harried. The crowds push their way in and out of shops, up and down alleys, crowding the walks, cutting across Commercial among the cars that can barely inch forward; but after the thunder and the shouting, the same street is silent on Sunday mornings. At this hour, shortly before ten a.m., suffused with soft, honey-colored light, sedate and empty, the spot has become a village again. The few people up are heading for St. Mary's of the Harbour, small groups standing in the church garden before the service starts.

The tight, grayish-white curls like a raffish bonnet, Norman Mailer strolls down Commercial alone past the church. ("Old What's-His-Name," Charley calls him, refusing to use it. "He's the Alfred Lord Tennyson of our time.") A sober senior citizen, deferential, shyish, minding his own business, he passes the garden. Does he nod? He comes close to it, passing these good Episcopalians. He cuts up to Bradford to buy his *Times* at Purdy's, a Sunday morning routine. In sandals, khaki shorts, the open shirt revealing more of that springy, if darker, steel-wool-like stuff at the chest. Unlike the Pilgrims' Monument, he is a cozy, unimposing landmark.

Julia opened the door. He reluctantly closed the book and put the pen down.

Julia after her shower in a terry cloth robe. They were both in their terry cloth robes, twins. The bureau mirror's dominance bothered him. They were both big, tall figures, prominently boned, square-shouldered, and in the mirror they resembled poster images. Oversize, elemental, imposing shapes. He turned off the overhead light.

She started to brush her hair, her head to one side. She was standing over him, watching him on the bed, obviously considering him, and he knew some comment was coming. "Here he is. Up here in your tower."

The sarcasm, he decided, might be good-natured. If he was lucky.

He wasn't. "And you're not dealing, as usual."

He felt impinged upon, pressed down on. "What do you want now, precisely?"

She didn't answer. The house after eleven was still active. A child coughed in the back, and someone used the bathroom. A window went up somewhere. "If *she* doesn't know how to deal with him, why should I?"

"Don't ask me. I'm not in this. Whose father are we talking about?"

"He's an old man, Julia."

"Oh, you *lie* to yourself about everything!" She put the brush down on the bureau. "Do you remember last summer? When Misty was making that stupid speech, out on the patio? You hugged her."

He was worrying about her voice carrying, and he lowered his.

"When everyone was drinking?"

"Yes, when everyone was drinking. You weren't *that* drunk yourself."

"*She* was. She just amused me because she was. She never is, and I hugged her. So what? That happened a year ago, and now you bring it up. Talk about being direct."

The priest's car pulled in behind the house, and the captain got out. He was whistling to himself in the dark, and then

Jerry could hear him urinating in the yard. He finally banged the tackle shed door shut.

"Well, I *didn't* think so much about it until you two decided to get chummy in New York."

"Julia? Listen. For the last time, please? For the absolute last time, will you? Please? She was visiting friends in Connecticut, and she came down to shop. You know how she turns up in New York two or three times a year. You know how she shops. We ran into each other, and we had dinner. That's it. That's all. Everything. Those are the facts."

"Oh, just *babes* in the city, weren't you? *Innocence,* I'll grant, and that's the trouble. You're smitten with her, at least a bit, but you even lie to yourself about it. You pretend it's not happening. You use up all your reserves keeping the truth away from yourself. You have no time for anything else. We haven't had sex in a month."

"A month? That's not true."

"Well, not since we came here."

He needed his own room back. There was something vibrating and busy about this place that made lovemaking seem out of character, an act that cut across the grain. "The walls are so thin," he said, half to himself.

"Well," she said, furious, just livid, "what if she *does* hear us? What is your mother going to do, in that case? Turn to stone on the spot?"

Ellen Maplewood knocked on the back door while Myra was getting the evening meal together. Ellen opened the door a bit, peering in, rubbing her shoes on the mat at the same time, trying not to track in sand. She was a veteran tenant, familiar with the place, and given to taking advantage. "I know a busy woman when I see one. I'll just be a minute."

Myra had her back to her and did not at first notice the company. "That's just about what I have." Then she turned.

Ellen Maplewood was a soft-featured, sharp-voiced little woman, no more than five feet two or three; the tall, white-haired professor towered above her majestically, like a cloud-capped peak. "I want you to meet our British houseguest,

Myra. I've told you about him, and I didn't want you to think we were holding out. We've just been settling in."

Myra shut off the tap and wiped her hands on her apron. "I always leave people alone until they're ready. I don't push. I don't pry." She had, in fact, seen the man about. She did not miss much. She could not afford to.

"Goodness! With us? You could have come down, you know. Professor Nickerson's an ornithologist. That's studying birds. He has come all the way up here to have a look at ours."

The scholar seemed not to know what to do with the sudden attention, and his modesty, Myra decided, was very British-like. "Oh, dear, really, but it's just Richard, please. We don't use titles much, nowadays, do we?"

Ellen looked severe. "That's earned, Dick, your due."

"Well, I'm sure I'm not used to them, am I?" He looked as if he might add something, some little courtesy, but could not think of what.

"Myra has a teacher in the family, too."

"Charley's a professor," Myra said, setting her straight. Charley was so high up he did not have many students, and every time he turned around he was getting another class off. "He's waiting now to hear about a grant. If he gets it, he won't have to teach. You'll have to meet all my sons, all professionals."

"We've been coming here so long, Dick. Like most who have one of Myra's cottages, we wouldn't think of going anywhere else. We all know each other, and you'll see what I mean when we're settled. We've had some perfectly marvelous patio parties. Wait until you meet the Donaldsons. Is that perfectly marvelous flutist back? He'll have to meet the flutist. Put us both down for the flutist."

Myra did what she did in her own good time and at her pace. She put her head at that reflective angle, ready to draw him out. "What birds are you going for?"

"Right now he's doing a paper on the bufflehead."

Myra decided that she was going to have to get him alone. "I know the terns, several kinds, but I don't think I would know a bufflehead."

"Oh, my!" Nickerson said, springing to life. "You have mergansers, goldeneyes, buffleheads and scaup in the sheltered inlets. You have waders in the salt marshes and bay flats. You have the black-breasted and semipalmated plovers, the knot, the dowitcher, the sanderling, the greater and lesser yellow-legs. You have the marbled godwit, the Judsonian curlew, the red phalarope and even a Baird's sandpiper, but these last are, of course, very rare, aren't they?"

Ellen was beaming. "You *see?* Didn't I just *tell* you he was a humbling experience!"

Myra fed the grandchildren first, and while the adults ate, the children watched television. The captain was watching TV these days, and he was in there with them. He would pull a chair up close to the screen, blocking their view. He settled in while they complained, having to shift positions. He ignored them. He particularly admired Wonder Woman, and when *she* came on, he expected quiet. The family in the dining room could hear him in the parlor, chuckling to himself. He would sometimes hoot and shout.

The family at the table tried to act as if all this were not transpiring. They largely ate in silence, and hurriedly, as if eager to finish, having important chores. Jerry still avoided the man as much as he could. Charley was more active in his defiance. He looked straight through him, as if he were not a solid mass. He was quiet these days. He certainly had nothing to say on the subject, but his drinking had picked up. He sat with a fresh drink in front of him now, beside his wineglass.

Myra chose a neutral topic. "That professor is veddy, veddy British."

Charley looked up, surprised. "That accent? He's *lived* here most of his life, Mother."

"When you're British, you're British. You don't forget."

Misty picked up her wineglass. She looked over it for a minute. "Merry England," she said bitterly, and Jerry looked up. "*We* did England once."

Charley frowned. "Why bring that up now?"

"Why not?"

Jerry looked at Charley. "Why? What happened?"

Nobody spoke for a moment. "Why can't we have a *pleasant* meal?" Myra asked. "Does anybody here know why not?"

Julia glanced at Misty. "Shall we vote?"

Myra had her head to the side, at her reflective angle. "The professor needs bringing out of himself."

"She's going to get a little patio group together again," Charley said. He looked around the table. "Right? I can spot it coming a mile off."

"I can produce the flutist. The professor could read from his paper. He's doing a paper."

Julia looked amused. "Oh? And on what, birds?"

Myra set her mouth. "We have no idea just how many birds we have on the Cape. I know I have not."

Jerry was thinking about the captain. Everyone was at the moment. "So. Who else is coming?" he asked, too innocently.

Myra could imagine the captain's taking over, shouting everyone down, monopolizing, loaded, loud, above the lot. "I haven't crossed all my bridges yet."

Charley glanced toward the parlor. "Which bridges are those now?"

She did not answer.

"I love the way everybody says what's on his mind around here," Julia said.

The captain appeared in the doorway. "Where's the Africans, Myra? Why ain't you showing off the Africans?" He could talk nonstop, but still did not miss much. "She's got Africans; now she's got Englishmen, too. Any kind of foreigner you want she can get." He stamped out, banging the kitchen door behind him.

Darwin flying in from Boston found a seat alone, but he didn't manage to keep the extra space. A small, plumpish, dark-haired woman sat down beside him, disturbing a cloud of department store cologne. She sat down first, then dragged several shopping bags in out of the aisle, against her feet.

"I thought I'd just slip over to Boston to shop," she said. She looked at him as if she were trying to place him. "I've been coming to the Cape for years without seeing Boston, without seeing much of anything else, in fact. When we get to the Cape, we tend to vegetate. Ned fishes, a bit, but I just unwind. I try to relax. This year, though, I promised myself I was going to see Boston. Do you know Boston? Well, on the whole, you can keep it.

"Oh, I'm Marion Cole, and I think we've met. We have one of Myra's cottages every summer. You're the artist in the family, aren't you? You've all been very successful in your chosen careers, haven't you, and I don't know how she's done it. Except for Lyle, of course, and everybody loves Lyle.

"We stay in that first small cottage at the bend, just past Myra's place. There isn't much room to move around in. We have Ned's mother with us this year, and I can't always get everything off my chest. I don't know why this didn't occur to me when Ned first suggested having her up, but I wanted to do something for the woman, and it just didn't. When I want to get something off my chest, Ned and I have dinner in town, dinner and drinks in some nice place, just the two of us, and then I have my say.

"The beach hasn't been very crowded this year. Do you remember the Canadians awhile back, when those little string suits were big? *Dark* people, weren't they? The women shouting at their children all day long in rapid-fire French. I have a little high school French—two years, in fact—but I couldn't follow that. There aren't many around at the moment. They say it's the falling exchange rate.

"When we came up early one year, before you boys arrived, an odd thing happened, and I don't suppose Myra's ever talked about it. She had an unexpected vacancy; the Donaldsons had canceled at the last minute. He needed an operation, and Myra took some Canadians in off the road. Well, Ned, Lyle and I were strolling on the beach when we ran into the woman's child, and sunning topless. She wasn't more than sixteen or seventeen. It was sunny that day, but chilly, like this, and she was lying close to the cliff. 'Like a little lost pearl,' Ned said, but I don't know about the pearl part. She certainly wasn't lost.

"Well, Lyle recognized her, and right off. 'That's cottage

three,' he kept saying, 'Yes, yes, yes, that's cottage three.' You know how he goes on. The whole thing bothered him. He didn't want to tell Myra, but you know Lyle. I said he had to. Well, Myra put a sweater on and went right over, and that was that. It didn't happen again, but Lyle got feeling pretty guilty about his part in it. He got very down about it, and then he had one of his little spells. I guess it was pretty serious, and Myra had him in Hyannis.

"I understand your father's back. Ellen Donaldson tells me stories, and believe me, she talks. She watches everything that goes on. Now he's your father, of course. I don't know what your thinking is on the subject. I don't pry, myself, but from what Ellen tells me, your mother has her hands full right now, what with the drinking and cleaning up. When is Lyle due in? How *he'll* take this, of course, she doesn't say. But you know your mother. The salt of the earth. A Christian, and there's so few. Never complains. Never says much. I don't know *how* she does it. 'Myra,' I've said, many times, 'what's your secret? I don't know how you stay so calm.' She never raises her voice, does she? She goes, you know, from morning to night."

Myra, Charley and Jerry met him at the airport. Darwin started asking questions before he was in the car.

"Oh, Marion Cole, Marion Cole, Marion Cole," Myra said, aloofly. "Anybody who listens to Marion Cole ought to have their head examined."

"*Mother!* I want some *facts!*"

"Now just a minute," Jerry said, sounding like Jason. "You're just in, and you're shouting."

"Nobody's taking a stand?"

"We've been looking into several retirement homes," Charley said wearily. "We've been in touch with several places."

Myra patted his knee. "Now I've got three of my sons back. I was thinking of some nice, fresh fish tonight."

"Who's *we*?" Jerry asked. "Charley has. Although I don't know how he thinks we're going to get him locked up."

"I just don't want to think about the problem, just yet. My! Isn't it a lovely day! Aren't you glad to be out of New York?"

"You aren't going to do anything, then? Just drift?"

"I don't see why you have to use that tone on her," Charley said.

"You artists," Myra said, "off in your world and temperamental. We don't expect them to come down to earth."

"He's young yet, anyway," Charley suggested. "Just thinks he has the answers."

The captain was climbing the front stairs when he had his first stroke. He fell several steps. Conscious, looking ashen, he could hardly speak. He called for a priest. Charley called for an ambulance. Hyannis kept him down there under observation.

He summoned the family. They trooped in to find him tied to equipment, and because he had been shaved, he hardly resembled himself. Without the baseball cap, the baldness showed. He looked raw and exposed. He cleared his throat. "I want to apologize for any inconvenience I have caused."

The priest patted his shoulder. "Now, Captain, God knows the human heart. It's there you'll be judged. These good people wouldn't want you to be too exacting on yourself."

"I am just saying what there is left *to* say," the captain said, without expression and looking straight ahead, "while there's time."

Everybody was quiet going out. Charley spoke first. "That's true, too. God *knows* what's in *his* heart."

"We shouldn't judge. I know I cannot."

"Well," Darwin said, "he'll be in there for a while, anyway, *pinned down*, Myra. So why don't you start thinking about your social life?"

Myra was working on the fourth cottage for the new tenants, the house she had hauled up from Wellfleet. Misty was in there now, making up beds. Everybody had chores, and Jerry felt at loose ends.

The soft drizzle outside covered his glasses, half obscuring his sight. He lowered his head, and the rolling moisture settled on his hair. The lumber lying beside the various cottages was darkened, drenched, there as it had been discarded through the years. He could smell a fresh pack of shingles waiting to go up. Important work stayed in abeyance, waiting for Lyle's return. She could make it without the others, but she could not make it without Lyle.

He saw Misty's head in the cottage window. When he had run into her in the city, she had something on her mind; she seemed to want to talk—hence his suggesting dinner—but, if so, she was quiet over the meal. He had taken her to a Greek restaurant in the East 30s in the middle of the week, and aside from a large group that appeared to be related to the management, the place had been empty. It had begun to snow, and when they emerged, the heavy, wet stuff was clinging to cornices, matting the silent streets. He had difficulty finding a cab.

"I like this kind of weather," she had said, taking his arm. "It's very comforting. You're very comforting."

She had seemed edgy in the restaurant, certainly not relaxed, and although he had wanted to lighten her spirits, he did not know that he had done anything. He said so. She just shook her head. Smiled mysteriously, as if he had accomplished more than he had guessed. "I suppose I've always been so sheltered," she said, a remark without apparent context.

She may have originated in the Middle West, but if she had been sheltered, she had been sheltered in the way that money shelters. There was a soft drink behind the family, what Charley called "Romanish soft drink funds," and when these wealthy Catholics went shopping, they hit San Francisco or New York. She now hit New York herself several times a year. In any case, she could deliver lines that, in anyone else, could be considered a brazen proposal, but she delivered them without their second meanings. "You make me feel all right, as if I don't *need* sheltering." Or *were* they merely bland? Who knew, with her?

The misting was turning to light rain. The screen door stuck at the top, and when he got that open, he found the door itself locked. He went around to the back, following the planking that led up to the stoop through the thorny undergrowth, a rusting portable grill half-buried in a spiky bush.

When he stepped inside, he stopped to wipe his glasses. Myra had this place, like all her places, filled with the kind of secondhand clutter that was meant to offer a homey touch or two: fussy, impractical lace curtains, clean but frayed at the edges; imitation lace doilies on the sagging, nubby couch with greenish fringe; a ceramic seahorse lamp with a pink shade; a wicker shelf with a dust-catching "display" of shells, small stones, seaglass and a powdery, ancient starfish that had actually come from Florida. A palm print also suggested other climes, her idea of more "color."

He could hear movements in the front bedroom, and when he reached the open doorway, she was making up the double bed in that sterile-looking cubicle filled with a metal bed, a huge maple dresser, and a standing lamp, its pull cord dangling with a fake gem. She looked up, pushed her hair back. Her skin glowed from bending. He studied the sparseness, the flaired facial bones. "Hi," she said. She tucked in the shapeless flannel shirt, the small breasts briefly evident, just hints.

"Jason just called. He and Lyle are on their way, in time for Lyle's birthday. Jason sounded very cheerful, but when he's being cheerful, he's telling you things haven't been all that upbeat. He has probably had his problems with Lyle, who doesn't travel well." He felt too light. He knew he was talking too much. "He'll keep all that to himself. Then, as his sense of abuse piles up, he'll let you know."

"*I* never know *half* the things that go on around here."

"Mother's busy right now. She claims she has work to do. She is pleased they're coming, but as long as she is working, she doesn't have to dwell on that. Dwell on pleasure. Happiness threatens her."

The sky suddenly opened up. The window was partly raised, the curtains sucked against the soaked screen. The rain bounced in small beads against the sill. He worked his way around the bed to shut the window. The rain enclosed them, sealing them off. "Lyle says he needs to keep busy. Come to think of it, *everybody* here needs to keep busy."

"Charley's drinking is a form of it."

What had she wanted to tell him? Charley, he supposed, could be having an affair. "I always wondered if he actually drinks more here."

"Not always, no."

He watched her slipping the pillows into fresh pillowcases. The rain was suddenly less frantic. It was coming down steadily now, pitting the sand, weighing the plum roses. "I've always wondered what you wanted to tell me in New York." He watched her fussing with the pillows, plumping them up, smoothing the spread. "Something was bothering you then."

"Was I going to tell you something?"

"Oh, yes."

She straightened. "Did you know Myra had been *married* before? When her mother died, when she wanted to get out of the house? She eloped with a high school sweetheart. Her father brought her back. He had it annulled. She's very close-mouthed, but then, when you're least expecting it, she'll tell you something you didn't *dream* of suspecting. I'm not supposed to tell anybody, of course. I haven't, either. She'd kill me if she knew I told you."

Myra had also told Julia, another woman. When Myra occasionally let her guard down, reached a confessional moment, she chose a woman for an audience, the less-trivial sex, fundamental victims.

"It is a wild, rank place, and there is no flattery in it," Thoreau remarked about the beach, but the observation fits Truro's backcountry: the abrupt, bare hills and gray poverty grass, the bogs and shallow pools, the hummocks and kettle bowls, the stubble, pitch pine and scrub oak, bent and twisted. The wind up there passing through sounds as if it's passing through rigging. The original cemetery is churchless now, and no flattery there. Deacon Hezeriah Purinton (1717) disintegrates under a death's head, crossed bones.

Charley walked in, and Jerry closed the notebook. Charley had been drinking and wasn't entirely focused. "I'll tell you what Misty didn't tell you in New York last winter. I'll give it to you straight, just in case you think life with her has been a piece of cake. I don't know why she didn't tell you herself. She's told everybody else. She's told her Avon lady, for instance, but they're pretty close. She serves her tea, and the two have these long, soul-searching talks. The woman, I think, is better than my therapist."

Jerry stood. "Charley . . ."

"Listen, you're going to like this. It has some touching parts. When we lost the child, we had a lot of problems, and we had family counseling. I finally got around to admitting to myself that I hadn't wanted another child, and when I did that, I had to face my guilt. I felt guilty most of the time, and I was generally off-balance. I wasn't as helpful as I should have been, and I didn't clearly see what I should have seen. She had bad dreams. She would wander the house afterward, still half-asleep. 'Someone's missing,' she'd call out, 'someone's missing. Who's missing?' Well, I felt blamed. I couldn't let myself off the hook. The therapist wasn't all that brilliant, considering what I know now, but he decided we needed some unstructured time together. She wasn't having orgasms, for one thing."

There was a movement in the hall, and Charley turned to check the door. He closed it more securely. "We went to London that spring during a sabbatical, and I decided I wasn't taking any books. When we landed in London, we tried in London, but we decided the city could be distracting, and we toured. We stayed in Shaftesbury, heading south, but no dice, not a dent. Then Lyme Regis. No luck. We stayed in Looe on the Cornish coast; not a bite. We stayed in Falmouth, and we tried there. We'd had a certain amount of drizzle on the trip, off and on, but the sky cleared near Falmouth. The sun came out, a dazzling two or three hours—a hopeful sign, I thought— but the break in the weather didn't help. We crossed to St. Ives. It didn't take in St. Ives. We stayed in Bideford, Devon, in Pilton, Somerset, and finally in Chipping Sodbury, just up the road. They do a nice tea in Chipping Sodbury, but tea is what we got. Then over to Oxford and back to London. Nothing, not a ripple. Everything quiet. We flew to Paris, a disaster, but by now I was buying books again. I couldn't see the point in not."

Jerry was standing at the window, his back to his brother. "I don't need to hear all this."

"I've just covered some of the fear; I haven't touched the pity yet. Well, we flew to New York, and we checked into another hotel, and now I'm coming to a major point: that hotel room. I don't suppose it was different from dozens of others, certainly not those in London or Paris, but its effect may have come from the accumulation. There was the modern city below the window, just beyond the drawn shade: jackhammers, car horns, the rattle of garbage cans, the clanging delivery trucks. But there had been something timeless about the being in the room, the human sitting on the bed in her slip, her bare feet touching the floor, knees together. She wasn't beautiful at that moment. She looked very tired. But indeed, the plainness, simplicity and regularity of the features increased the impression, the simple eternality of the figure, the human with its troubles.

"I suddenly glimpsed my murderous self-centeredness. Oh, I'd told her before that she couldn't blame herself for the miscarriage, but this time, you see, I was just offering reassurance, not asking for it. I told her I loved her, I'd always loved her and always would. 'I didn't *have* a miscarriage,' she said. 'I had an abortion.' Because she had decided, in some kind of fit, that if I didn't want her child, she didn't want mine."

Jerry was still standing at the window. The tide was in, the bay gathering the darkness, and a sail's slant hovered in the distance. Flute music was coming from the Donaldsons' place in the fading light. Marion Cole's mother-in-law appeared on their stoop. The old lady generally seemed ordinary enough, but whenever she heard the flute music, she burst into a hymn. "Bringing in the sheaves," she sang now, over the Mozart piece, "bringing in the sheaves."

"Well, we've had our troubles before, Jerry. Who hasn't? But *this* duplicity was appalling, *just* appalling. Do you *see* what she'd been doing? She'd kept it from me, and all that time, all that time—living in the same house, eating at the same table, sleeping in the same bed. And *now* where was I? What's safe? What goes on in her head? What goes on in *anybody's* head? Who knows? I don't know, anymore," he said.

"We shall come rejoicing," Mrs. Cole's mother-in-law continued, in a clear, true voice, over the Mozart, "bringing in the sheaves."

When the hospital released the captain, he got himself dressed in seconds flat. He buttoned his flannel shirt quickly, patted the forgotten cigars in his top pocket, and put his baseball cap on last, pushing it down over the bald spot.

The nurse appeared with the doctor's prescriptions, delaying him. He didn't need them. He was released, wasn't he? And if he was sick, then he shouldn't be released. *Make up your mind,* he thought, without saying it, because he didn't want to stay in there arguing all day. He put the written prescriptions in his pocket behind the cigars.

"Who's picking you up?" she asked, as if there were some law about that. "Have you got people waiting?" She was a jug-shaped little woman with a hard face.

He knew that Myra was not. He had not mentioned his release because he wanted to get to town first, to celebrate, then surprise her later. "I got connections," he said mysteriously, fixing her with his piercing, squint-eyed look.

He also decided that he did not need that talky priest, and when he got downstairs, he called a cab. He had brushed against the Wings of Death, and as he had expected, the encounter had not shaken him overmuch.

When he told the driver that he wanted to go to Provincetown, the man turned around to look at him while he was putting the handle down on the meter. He seemed mildly curious. "Do you live there, Sport, or are you just seeing the sights?" he asked.

"No, I don't live there, and it doesn't have any *sights* for me *to* see," he said. He unwrapped his first cigar. "Been all over the world, including Provincetown. I ain't a boy."

The driver was going to be talky, like that priest. "I gave up cigars when I couldn't get cigars from Cuba. They spoil you."

"Well, I ain't a Cuban," the captain said.

"I was in Cuba, before Castros." He shook his head. "Now you talk about your night life. That was night life. You ever been to Cuba?"

The captain was not used to being questioned directly, not outside a hospital. "Cuba wasn't a place I ever cared to see," he said sullenly, very formally. He sat back with his cigar. "Surprised me even a Com-nist would want it. Ain't they got better places to take over?"

"What the pope gives up, the Communists grab."

"He didn't want it. Not that I have always seen eye-to-eye with him, either."

That last observation apparently settled him down. He turned on his radio and sat back himself, concentrating on the driving, the thing he was paid to do. The captain didn't have to discuss the affairs of the day with a cab driver. He had more on his mind than that.

When the cab reached Bradford Street, the air was just turning hazy and the evening traffic was picking up, not bumper-to-bumper yet, but on its way. He got out and cut down an alley. He decided to steer clear of the milling tourists on Commercial Street and stay in the alleys.

The bars were stirring. He paused at the first, originally somebody's home. He climbed the steps onto the porch. He wandered in without knowing about the door charge, but was soon stopped. "They charge for everything around here," he said, getting his wallet out, "including the doors."

The attendant was sympathetic. "Isn't that the gospel truth."

While the boy was making change, the captain lit his dead cigar. He took it out of his mouth and studied it wisely. "Them Com-nists got all the Catholics working for them now, rolling the best cigars. The pope's lost the cigar business. You ever been to Cuba?"

"I haven't been anywhere," the boy said, walking off.

The captain mounted the barstool but could not see too clearly in the dimness. The air was filled with heavy, overbearing sweetish smoke. He thought at first that the singer in the low-cut gown was a woman, and when he realized that it was not, he felt a little off-balance. He looked around to see if anyone had noticed. He ordered a drink, deciding to engage the bartender. "Nothing new here," he said. "Nothing I ain't seen before. Have been all over the world. Have come home to die."

"That so?" the bartender said, having heard them all. "Well, I guess we all go."

He wasn't sure what he thought about this place. He could

not find the good places anymore, but on the other hand, he had never much bothered with the town before. He had been a family man who had pretty much limited his drinking to a bottle on the premises. That is, up until now.

He studied the two men on his left at the bar, a white and a black. "Africans," he observed, trying to draw them into conversation. "She's got Africans and Englishmen, too. She doesn't need me. Used to be, though, you could go home and get yourself a beer."

They turned, mildly curious. The white was big, but bald. He had shaved his head. Some of the fuzz was starting to come back, and while he listened, he rubbed his palm over the spot. He wore a leather motorcycle jacket, studded more than usual, and a garish purple headband. "That isn't beer you're into now, Pop," he said, looking down at the captain's glass. "You think you can handle that rum neat?"

The captain frowned. "Nothing I ain't tried to drink, and drank it. Been all over the world, been to the four corners, have sailed the Seven Seas, and so there is nothing new I need to learn."

The black looked more intelligent. He was wearing several chains, and a gold loop dangled from his left ear. He was also big, but without fat. His bare biceps glistened in the half-light. "We have a sailor here, evidently," he said.

The captain bent around the fat white to examine the black's gold loop. "What's that you got in your ear? You African, too?"

They looked at each other. "He's *tribal*, man, true blue," the white said, "and from the deepest parts."

"Pretty deep," the black admitted.

"What do you mean by that—'pretty deep'? You're *very* deep, and you know it."

The captain bought his second rum, then started on it, just to show that it could be done. When he got his wallet out, the two exchanged glances.

"We're close," the black said, still looking at the white. "We're very recently business partners."

The white was still playing with the bald spot on his head

where the fuzz was starting to grow back. "Oh, yes, we're in the wheelchair business. And the van business."

"The van was thrown in. We have recently acquired the wheelchairs," the black said. "Let's drink to the wheelchair business." He had a low, soothing voice and did not have to raise it. He had no accent, either, and the captain was beginning to think that they had all been educated out of it.

The white raised his beer in the air without drinking it. "What's your business, Pop?"

"He told you," the black said, "but you don't listen. You have a habit of not listening, Jake. He's a sailor."

The captain's vision was beginning to spin in the smoke, and he put his cigar out. "I'm now retired, since I have seen everything anyways. Seen what there is to see. And I don't need that talky priest to show me. He ain't seen everything. He don't know that much."

The black leaned around the white. "You loose from some home around here, Admiral?"

His face darkened and he grew thoughtful for a moment. "I've got a wife," he explained with some dignity, "but we don't see eye to eye."

The black finished his beer. "A common problem, easily recognized," the black said, putting his glass back down on the bar. "Right, Jake?"

"Eye to eye?" the white asked. "That's always asking a lot. "An eye *for* an eye, more likely."

"She's in the real estate business. She can rent you anything you want. She's got herself more cottages up there in Truro than I can count." His head was spinning again, and he looked away from the room. "More, at least, than I *care* to count."

"I know Truro," the white said. He nodded to himself. "A pretty spot."

The captain put his glass down in front of him, then shoved it farther aside. He was trying to keep his thoughts steady. He had more to say. "It ain't much. I can't see the water up there. She's got the bay, but that ain't the ocean. It ain't actually *water*."

The black agreed. "It isn't the Seven Seas, is it?"

"I think I could use some air," the captain said.

The white climbed down from the barstool. "That's the ticket. We could take you around," he suggested, looking at the black but talking to the captain. "Maybe we could find you a gold loop like his. You ever have your ears pierced? Show him the ropes. And maybe show you something you haven't seen yet."

The room was beginning to distance itself, and the voice wasn't coming through too clearly. "I'll just be getting along."

They accompanied him across the room, toward the door. "Sure," the white said, "you bet."

They stepped into a mild, invisible drizzle in the dark. The captain had hoped that the air would clear his head, but the alley was by now jammed with people, and he could not get any of it. He felt cold and started to sweat. "I need my pills," he said. "I got to get my pills."

The big black put his arm around the captain's shoulder, supporting him, a numbing grip. "We know where we can get you some. That's all you want. Right, Jake?"

While the black continued to lend support, they crossed the alley. Then threaded their way through a crowded pizza parlor past a beaded doorway into a back room stacked with empty pizza cartons. A clerk followed, a blond, bare-chested boy wearing a short apron around his middle, but little else.

The black released his grip for a moment. "The admiral's buying the pills. The admiral's treat."

The boy watched while the captain fumbled with his wallet. "I haven't got all day," he said, holding out his hand.

The first pain hit the side of his face. The captain dropped his wallet. "I need help," he said in a low voice. "I need the priest."

The white looked at the black. "We aren't going too near any priests tonight, Pop, and we still have to get your ears pierced."

The drizzling had ceased, and the evening sky was clear. The air smelled fresh and gusty. The tide was up, and working in the kitchen with the window open, Myra could hear it slapping the rocks below. Jason was back with Lyle and his two boys. The party was starting. The guests had begun to file onto the patio.

While there was all that activity out there, in *his* honor, Lyle paced around the kitchen underfoot, biting his nails, trying to sort through his anxieties. He would choose one, reject that, and start another. "Yes, yes, yes. I liked the trip, yes. Too much *traveling*, though. Do you know what I mean, Ma? Too many things to see. And hot, yes. Florida's *hot*. Too many people. Good to get out, I guess, but good to get back. Do you know what I mean? You got a lot of people out there, though, Ma, haven't you? That's a big crowd, yes."

She scratched the back of her neck, the paring knife still in her hand. She was trying to peel potatoes for the salad. She had got a late start. She was behind schedule, and as usual, always at this point, she wondered why she had invited all those people. Why had she bothered? "I don't know why you aren't out there. I don't know why you're hanging around in here."

He was going through the bread box, looking for donuts, his back to her. He couldn't find them, but there was a piece of sponge cake left. He unwrapped the plastic foil, then balled it up in his free hand. "I wanted to talk to you, for Christ sakes! Don't I have *news* to tell? Did you get all my cards? Anything new happen here?"

"That's your party out there. It's your birthday, isn't it? What would you say if I had forgotten?"

He turned around, his mouth still filled with cake. "I don't mean the *family*, Ma, no. I need to see the family." He stopped in his tracks. "I said that Jason couldn't get me home in time for my birthday, but he did. Right? He did," he said, wiping his palms off on his pants. "I was wrong. I admit it."

Standing at the sink, her hands plunged in the cold water, feeling around for the potatoes, she did not actually hear the van pulling around to the rear of the house, partly because the noise had picked up on the patio. She couldn't hear the tide now, either. From the kitchen window, though, she saw the van there, suddenly materialized. She froze. She had had *him* on her mind all evening. Although the van could be lost, more tourists wandering around in the dark, she could not help connecting it with the captain. She had that sense. She had always had.

Lyle shook his head, his expression changing. "But his *driving*, Ma! *Jesus!* Did you know that Jason drove that way? Did you? Did you? Yes, yes, yes! His *kids* in the car, too!"

Charley appeared from the patio, banging the side door. He had been drinking since five, and his face was flushed, his gait unsteady. "Who's in charge of the fire?"

Lyle smacked the side of his face. "I'm in charge of the fire. I almost forgot. Don't touch the fire, Charley. No, no, no! Don't touch the fire. There's a lot of *wind* out there. Sparks can fly."

"What wind? What sparks? It's going out."

Lyle left ahead of him. "I'm in charge, I'm in charge, everybody! Yes, yes, yes! Don't touch the fire. Don't touch the fire, kids!"

Myra was left alone at the sink, staring at the handicap van. She saw someone steer a wheelchair down the ramp and park it in the backyard. The figure climbed back into the van and reversed it quickly. It left before she could get her hands dried. She could just make out the form in the chair in the dimness, but even from that distance, she suspected she knew who was in the chair. She was running on some level not usually used, and all her senses were alerted. However, she still did not move.

Coming up late behind the house with a covered dish, Marion Cole had seen the same thing. The details had not been spared. She knocked at the back door with the side of her hand, trying to hold the bulky dish against her chest at the same time. She could not get a firm grip because of the flimsy pot holders. She finally lowered the dish down onto the stoop. "Myra? Myra? Are you in there?" She was trying to keep her voice down, and confidential. "There's something out here I think you should be aware of."

Myra came out on the stoop. "I am," she said, drying her hands. "I can see, can't I?"

The dead man's arms hung limply over the sides of the chair. The studded leather jacket was too long in the sleeves, and the pale fingers barely showed. A gold loop dangled from his left ear. The head was back, showing off the purple headband. The revealed throat was bloodless, like the fingers. The wheelchair's slender metal frame shone in the hazy half-light. The canvas back bulged slightly against the body's weight.

Marion Cole looked galvanized. "Have you called the police?" As she spoke, she was still staring at the chair.

Myra did not yet know just what she was going to do, but once the question was there, the challenge laid down, she felt the stupor shift, move just a little. She knew what she was not going to do. "I'm not calling the police."

Marion Cole heard the tone. She finally looked directly at Myra. "We could get one of the men, then."

At that moment the noise on the patio increased. She could hear Charley arguing with Jason, and then Lyle's voice above the others, still worrying about his fire. "What's keeping Ma?" he asked. "Where's Ma?"

"Men? What men?"

"Why, my goodness, you have five boys. Myra, dear, we all have to learn to lean sometimes."

Myra wasn't listening. As far as she was concerned, she was alone. She had always been so. She had her head to the side, in the reflective angle, the level that tuned out the world. "I have guests," she told herself. "I have a house filled with people. I have my obligations."

Marion Cole said nothing. She was going to remember that peculiar look for the rest of her life.

Myra studied the tackle shed. Then the long, intense gaze included the chair. "You know" she said, still talking to herself, "he'll wheel right up there."

Marion wasn't following the reasoning. "I still say we should call the authorities."

Myra gripped the handles. The chair seemed to respond on its own, ready to move anywhere. The complicity reassured her. "I'll cross that bridge when I come to it. Right now, though, we're all going to have a *pleasant* evening."

Marion gradually understood. The woman's will was finally spellbinding, and under that spell, feeling frozen, she could feel herself retreat from the moment. She grew reflective in defense. "You have always managed, haven't you, Myra?"

Myra did not answer. When she reached the shed door, she came to a short step, then a turn, and she had to shove. The captain looked as fierce as ever, as if about to object.

Marion watched from a safe distance, her hands on her hips, her neck and back stiff, as if about to break if she did not change positions. She could not. In fact, she did not know *how* the woman had managed. "You never crossed him once, did you? You never raised your voice. I've always had to have my say. I have to get things off my chest."

Myra shut the door and came back down the step. "Well, I'm not built that way. I don't judge. I never could. I have just learned to keep things bottled up."

Around the other side of the house, Lyle had the grill going on the patio. The air was permeated with woodsmoke; the fish was grilling, and the flute music had started.

Marion Cole's mother-in-law was in rare form. "Oh, Jerusalem, my happy home," she sang above the background music, a Vivaldi piece, "when shall I come to thee?" The voice was in perfect pitch.